### *"I take long showers," Rex said.*

"In the morning or evening?" Lisa asked.

"Morning."

"Then we shouldn't have a problem sharing. I bathe at night."

"With bubble bath and scented candles, I'll bet." Rex suspected that she had fancy bottles everywhere.

"Soaking in the tub relaxes me."

"There's nothing wrong with that. It's actually kind of sexy."

"Oh." Lisa angled her head, making her perfectly coiffed bob tilt to one side. "Then thank you, I guess."

"Sure."

Neither of them said anything after that, and the room seemed to shrink even more. He could actually feel them breathing the same air. She was almost close enough to kiss.

Dear Reader,

I would like to thank all of you who take the time to send fan letters to your favorite authors.

Over the years, I've received some very special fan letters. In fact, I received an amazing e-mail today. A reader from England wrote to tell me about a British-based book club that read the 2008 Mills and Boon release of *Always Look Twice* (my 2005 Silhouette Bombshell). According to the letter, they all believe that "Agent West is the greatest hero in the history of fiction," and some of the book club members may be working on an Agent West fan site.

I'm honored and awed that one of my heroes stirred this kind of reaction! It's great timing, too, because Agent West plays a minor role in *Protecting Their Baby*. He tends to crop up now and then, reappearing as the FBI guy that he is.

And speaking of heroes, Rex Sixkiller, the male protagonist in *Protecting Their Baby*, was inspired by a reader of Cherokee descent who offered to let me borrow the Sixkiller name. I kept the name in the back of my mind, waiting for the right character to embody it.

That said, I love hearing from my readers. You are the reason I write.

Best,

*Sheri WhiteFeather*

# SHERI WHITEFEATHER
## *Protecting Their Baby*

Silhouette®

Romantic
SUSPENSE

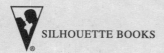

SILHOUETTE BOOKS

Recycling programs
for this product may
not exist in your area.

ISBN-13: 978-0-373-27660-8

PROTECTING THEIR BABY

Visit Silhouette Books at www.eHarlequin.com

**Printed in U.S.A.**

**Books by Sheri WhiteFeather**

Silhouette Romantic Suspense

*Mob Mistress* #1469
*Killer Passion* #1520
*\*Imminent Affair* #1586
*\*Protecting Their Baby* #1590

Silhouette Bombshell

*Always Look Twice* #27
*Never Look Back* #84

Silhouette Desire

*Sleeping With Her Rival* #1496
*Cherokee Baby* #1509
*Cherokee Dad* #1523
*The Heart of a Stranger* #1527
*Cherokee Stranger* #1563
*A Kept Woman* #1575
*Steamy Savannah Nights* #1597
*Betrayed Birthright* #1663
*Apache Nights* #1678
*Expecting Thunder's Baby* #1742
*Marriage of Revenge* #1751
*The Morning-After Proposal* #1756

*Warrior Society

## SHERI WHITEFEATHER

is a bestselling author who has won numerous awards, including readers' and reviewer's choice honors. She writes a variety of romance novels for Silhouette. She has become known for incorporating Native American elements into her stories. She has two grown children who are tribally enrolled members of the Muscogee Creek Nation.

Sheri is of Italian-American descent. Her great-grandparents immigrated to the United States from Italy through Ellis Island, originating from Castel di Sangro and Sicily. She lives in California and enjoys ethnic dining, shopping in vintage stores and going to art galleries and museums. Sheri loves to hear from her readers. Visit her Web site at www.SheriWhiteFeather.com.

To Lisa, my sister's dance teacher in Oregon—
here's to hot guys and red high heels!

# Chapter 1

*I'm screwed,* Rex Sixkiller thought.

He should have known that Lisa Gordon was going to spell trouble. He'd pegged her as a good girl from the start. Then again, she had gotten dirty that night.

Yeah, with the help of extra-dirty martinis.

He stared at Lisa. She was seated across from him in his L.A. office, and he'd never been so scared in all in his thirty-six years. Yes, *him.* A decorated Desert Storm veteran, a licensed private investigator and a Warrior Society activist.

"Are you sure?" he asked.

She responded with a jerky nod. She looked like

the good girl she was, with a blond bob and innocent blue eyes. Her long, lean, sinful body was
another matter. Of course she was a dance instructor who owned her own studio, so her knockout
figure was well earned. She looked the same as the
night he'd met her at the bar.

She twisted her hands on her lap. "I did one of
those home tests, and then I saw a doctor to confirm
the results." Another twist. Another nervous reaction.

He wished they were back at the bar. He could
use a stiff belt about now. "So much for the protection, huh?"

She went clinical. "The doctor said that if a condom is used correctly, the chance of becoming
pregnant is less than three percent. If used incor-
rectly, a twelve percent chance occurs." Her breath
hitched. "Maybe we did something wrong."

He shook his head. He never got sloppy with a
rubber, not even after a couple of drinks. Besides,
Lisa had been tipsy that night, not him. "The condom probably had a defect we weren't aware of."

A baby-making leak, he thought. How else could
his little swimmers have gotten through?

In the silence, an uncomfortable connection
passed between them, a reminder of their one-night
stand, of sizzling sex and an awkward morning after. In the light of day, it had become apparent they

had absolutely nothing in common. He remembered how they'd politely exchanged phone numbers, with no intention of ever calling each other.

And now here she was, six weeks later, pregnant with his child.

"Are you planning to keep it?" he asked, even though he already knew the answer. Why else would she approach the father? A practical stranger? An abortion would be simpler without him.

"Yes, I'm going to have this baby." To emphasize her point, she placed a protective hand over her still-flat stomach. Then she said, "But I did consider adoption."

He leaned forward in his chair. He was seated behind his desk, and she was on the other side of the wooden barrier. "You did?"

She nodded. "I'm adopted, and I have an amazing family. But I'm ready to be a mom. I think I'll be good at it."

Rex didn't have an amazing family. He'd watched his parents bitch and bicker. Sometimes they used to direct their frustration at him—the product of an unplanned pregnancy and forced marriage. They should have gotten divorced, but they were still together, miserable as ever. Rex had decided long ago that he would never get married, and it was a vow he intended to keep.

Not that Lisa expected him to marry her, but he still feared that he was on the verge of losing his freedom. Rex worked hard, but he played hard, too. He had no idea how a child was supposed to fit into his lifestyle.

"I understand if you want a paternity test after the baby is born," she said. "But just so you know, I haven't been with anyone in almost a year, except for you."

"I believe you." He didn't doubt that the baby was his. He'd been a P.I. long enough to rely on his instincts, and Lisa was as honest as Abe Lincoln's reputation. He would have preferred to pin it on another guy, but he couldn't.

"I appreciate that you trust me."

He shrugged, waited a beat, and then said, "I don't think I'm going to be a very good father. But I'll do the best I can," he added quickly.

What else could he say? He couldn't very well tell her to buzz off and leave him alone. He was a bit more honorable than that.

A bit...

Lisa seemed to be analyzing his bad-dad remark and debating if she should comment on it. Luckily, she skipped it, saying instead, "I think it's important for a child to have two committed parents, but I would have raised this baby alone if I had to. If you'd..."

Refused to accept responsibility, he thought. If only he could, if only he had it in him to walk away. "If we're going to share a kid, then we'll have to work on getting to know each other."

"Yes, we will."

She started wringing her hands, much in the way she'd done earlier. Apparently she was nervous about getting to know him. Clearly, he wasn't her usual type. Clearly, she'd misbehaved that night.

Dirty martinis and dirty sex.

And on her thirtieth birthday, no less. Rex considered the tiny life in her womb and winced accordingly. Was this the Creator's idea of a joke? A gift for her big three-oh?

Once again, silence stumbled between them. They were off to a hell of start with this getting-to-know-each-other thing. She wasn't his usual type, either.

Still, on that fateful night, they'd flirted shamelessly. They'd even fed each other shelled peanuts and kissed on the dance floor.

By the time the bar closed, they'd been desperate for more. He'd invited her back to his condo, and she'd readily accepted. Of course she hadn't been totally irresponsible. She'd gotten his name and address from his ID and given it to her girlfriends, just in case he was an ax murderer and she was never heard from again.

He'd promised her friends that he would be good to her. Now he wondered if those same friends knew about the baby and if they blamed themselves for letting the birthday girl go home with a stranger.

Not that they could have stopped her. She was an adult, capable of making up her own mind.

Her own *intoxicated* mind.

Damn, he thought. Did that even count?

"I should go." Lisa cut into the quiet, preparing to leave. "I have some errands to run."

Rex glanced up from his desk. "I'll walk you out." Somehow it seemed like the right thing to do, even if allowing her to make a hasty retreat would've been easier.

"I parked down the street and around the corner."

"No problem." Parking spots in this area were difficult to come by. She was lucky she'd found one relatively close.

He opened the office door for her, and they walked side by side. She smoothed her blouse, a pretty white garment tucked into a slim black skirt. She looked sleek and professional. He wondered how long it would take for her to develop a bump and if people were going to refer to him as the "baby daddy." Wasn't that the phrase of the day? The thing to say?

The spring weather was warm and bright, and the

city was active and noisy. As he and Lisa rounded the corner and headed down a small side street, she pointed out her car.

She drove a vintage Mustang, but he wasn't surprised by her vehicle of choice. While they'd chatted at the bar, she'd told him that her grandfather restored old cars.

"I'll probably get something newer when the baby comes," she said. "Maybe an SUV."

A kid car, Rex thought. Already she was turning into a soccer mom.

"But there's still time." She managed a smile. "I've got a ways to go."

Would he be even more scared by then? Or would it get easier? "A friend of mine is going to be a dad soon. His kid is due sometime this month. He's married, though." A point that made their situations nothing alike. "He teaches close-quarter combat, and his wife is a homicide detective."

"Wow." Lisa stood beside her car. "That's going to be one tough little baby."

"Tough and sweet. They're having a girl."

"A girl would be nice. Or a boy," she added, referring to the baby she'd made with Rex. "I don't have a preference."

Neither did he, other than wishing the condom hadn't failed. Uncomfortable, he shifted his feet.

She fell silent, too, and they went back into awkward mode.

How long would it take for them to have a relaxed conversation? To feel normal around each other?

"I'll call you after my next doctor appointment," she said. "Just to let you know how things are going."

"Sure. Okay." He supposed it was a place to start, even if he wasn't prepared for any of it.

She unlocked her car and opened the door. But as she turned to climb behind the wheel, she froze in her tracks.

And let out a blood-curdling scream.

On the front seat of her car was a doll that resembled a newborn, only its rounded little body was mangled, with broken limbs and unblinking eyes staring into nothingness. In the center of its tiny chest, where its heart would be, was a knife.

Equally horrified, Rex reached for Lisa, pulling her away from the gruesome sight and into his arms.

While he held her, while she burst into fear-drenched tears, he called the police, reporting what appeared to be the mock murder of their unborn child.

Lisa couldn't seem to let go of Rex. Nor could she stop crying. Who would do something so sick? So cruel?

Finally, she got the strength to step back and wipe her tears. But she couldn't stop from staring at Rex, and in between her shivers, she fixated on his eyes.

The doll had brown eyes, too, and a tuft of dark hair. Was that how their baby was going to look?

"I don't understand." Her voice echoed in her head, the sound thick and hoarse. "Why is this happening?"

"I don't know," came the concerned reply. "But I won't let anyone hurt you or the baby."

Would he be able to protect her? He couldn't be with her every moment of the day. They barely knew each other. Still, she wanted to believe him, to take his promise at face value.

"You're awfully pale," he said, as they waited for the police.

"Sometimes I faint." She clenched her middle. "But it's normal early on."

Rex seemed ready to catch her if she fell. He was certainly more stable than she was.

"Do you need to sit down?" he asked.

"I should be okay." She removed a small bottle of water from her purse and took a sip. "This may help."

"You're not going to pass out?"

She shook her head. A moment later, she feared that she'd spoken too soon. She got dizzy. "I think maybe…"

Rex moved in to grab her. She didn't lose consciousness, but she clung to him for support, her senses on alert. He smelled fresh and clean, like a walk in the woods. It was his cologne. She remembered it from before. Thank goodness she still found his fragrance appealing. Since the pregnancy, some previously pleasant scents roiled her stomach.

Everything about him was appealing: the width of his shoulders, his height, his stunning cheekbones, the short, sleek thickness of his straight dark hair.

Before she got too attached, she took a deep breath and severed their contact, standing on her own again.

On the night of her birthday, she'd taken an uncharacteristic risk by going home with him, and now she was carrying his child.

A child someone had threatened to kill.

Anxious for the police to arrive, she glanced toward her Mustang. She didn't wonder how the door had been unlocked and then relocked. A wire hanger or a slim jim or whatever those devices were called would've done the trick. Vintage cars were easy to access.

Lisa took another sip of water. Rex was watching her, and his concerned scrutiny made her self-conscious. He reached out to smooth a strand of hair away from her cheek, where it stuck to the slight dampness of her skin. She suspected that she had mascara streaks running down her face, too.

The police finally showed up. One of them, a stout detective named Bell, eyed Rex.

"Don't I know you?" the detective asked.

Rex nodded. "You worked on a case that involved some friends of mine. Daniel Deer Runner and Allie Whirlwind."

"Oh, that's right. You and Deer Runner are part of the same Warrior Society." Bell gathered information while his partner processed the crime scene. "So, what's going on here? What's the significance of the doll?"

Rex responded, "Lisa is pregnant."

The detective opened his notepad. "Are you the father?"

"Yes. She just told me about it today." The P.I. explained his whereabouts, being in his office with Lisa, then walking her to her car.

Bell tapped his pen. "Do all of you Society guys have women who are being threatened?"

"She isn't my woman," came the candid response. "It was just one night."

"I see."

Bell glanced at Lisa, but didn't say anything to her. While he interviewed Rex, she wondered what the Warrior Society reference meant. Did Rex belong to a club or organization? And what was the deal about their women being threatened? She didn't like the sound of that.

She stole a glance at the doll. The other detective was taking pictures of it.

Soon Bell left Rex to his own devices and interviewed Lisa. He spoke gently, as if trying to put her at ease. Did he think she might break? That she was as fragile as her appearance? Now she wished that she hadn't cried.

When he asked her who she thought could have done this, she was at a loss. She didn't have any enemies, at least not that she knew of. The questions continued, but she wasn't much help.

"Maybe somebody saw something," Lisa said, even though the side street was mostly back lots and alleyways.

"We'll be looking for witnesses," Bell assured her.

She glanced at Rex. By now, he was jotting down license plate numbers of other parked cars.

Bell followed the line of her sight. "Your friend is going to conduct his own investigation. But he'll be sharing information with us, too."

It seemed odd to hear the father of her child being referred to as a friend. But it was as good a description as any. "He offered to protect me."

"Then maybe you should let him."

A short time later, she and Rex were dismissed, and they returned to his office, leaving her vehicle for the police to finish examining.

Once they were inside the Sixkiller Investigations building, Rex said, "I want you to come home with me."

Déjà vu, she thought. She'd heard those words from him once before. But this time she assumed it was because he wanted to talk about the case.

"If you're not up for the drive, you can ride with me," he said. "After your car is released, I can arrange to have it brought to my place."

"I can drive." She needed to prove that she had inner strength, no matter how frightened or exhausted she was. "But first, there's something I need to know." She looked into his eyes, trying not to be become fixated on them again. "What's a Warrior Society?"

He held her gaze. "In my case, it's an intertribal group of former military men who defend American Indian rights."

"So, it's an activist organization?"

"Yes."

She should have known that Rex wasn't a passive man, that his Native roots defined him. Instinctively, she touched her tummy. Her baby was going to be part...

Part what? She didn't even know what tribe Rex

was from. Up until now, she hadn't considered the cultural differences between them.

She questioned him again. "Why did Detective Bell make that comment about women being threatened?"

"Because he worked on a Warrior Society–related case that involved a stalking. But it's unlikely this situation is related to my activism. I only found out about the baby today. It's doubtful that someone associated with me would have known that you were pregnant."

"Maybe they saw us in the bar. Maybe they've been following me ever since."

"Hoping we would reconnect? I haven't seen you since that night. We haven't even talked on the phone. Tailing you to get to me wouldn't have made much sense."

"So you think that whoever did this is associated with me?"

"Yes, but I'm going to investigate every angle. I won't rule out a Society connection, not until I know for sure."

Lisa didn't know what to think, if the baby was being threatened because of her or because of its father.

Either way, she agreed to go with him. Because going home alone didn't seem like a very good option.

# Chapter 2

After the police released Lisa's car, she followed Rex to his house, and the entire time she was in traffic, the knifed doll loomed in her mind. She'd never been so grateful when his complex came into view.

He offered her a seat on his leather sofa. The condo was decorated in dark woods and masculine fabrics. Laminate floors, textured walls and floor-to-ceiling windows provided contemporary ambience. The balcony in his bedroom overlooked the pool. She remembered the view.

"Are you hungry?" he asked.

"A little." She knew that she needed to eat.

"Is Chinese okay? I can have it delivered."

"That's fine."

He rummaged through a kitchen drawer and retrieved a take-out menu. She chose an entrée and handed it back to him.

While he ordered the food, she noticed the magazines on his coffee table, which ranged from sports publications to men's entertainment—the kind with centerfolds.

But what did she expect from a free-wheeling bachelor?

"Do you have a theory about all of this?" she asked.

He sat beside her. "All of this?" He made a grim expression. "You mean, the threat? I think the perpetrator is angry at you for getting pregnant."

"Do you think he or she is trying to scare me into having an abortion?"

"Probably."

There was no way she was going to terminate her pregnancy. "And if I don't? Then what? Will this person—this perpetrator—try to make me miscarry? Or attempt to kill the baby after it's born?"

He put his hand on her knee. "I won't let it go that far."

Lisa hoped he was able to live up to his claim. She wanted to feel safe, but at the moment, she was still scared. At least Detective Bell seemed to think that Rex was capable of the job. That gave her a measure of comfort.

He frowned. "You still look pale. Do you need to lie down before the food comes?"

On the sofa? Or in a guest room? Surely not in his room. Last time when she'd awakened beside him, naked as the day she was born, she'd turned shy. She remembered tugging at the sheet and struggling for something to say.

"Lisa?" he pressed, reminding her that she hadn't answered his question. He even squeezed her knee.

"I don't need to lie down."

"You sure?"

"Yes." Disturbed by her memories, her muscles tensed.

He was astute enough to quit touching her. He removed his hand from her leg. He paused before he said, "I'd like to interview you. But it can wait until after we eat."

"That's fine." She suspected that he would be repeating Detective Bell's questions, along with a vast number of his own. She had no idea how personal the interview would get, but she prepared herself for the worst.

Not that she had anything to hide. She lived in a cozy old house, enjoyed the chaos that came with running a dance studio and spent Sundays with her family.

Not exactly the kind of life that lent itself to deranged threats.

Their meals were delivered, and he shoved the magazines aside, toppling a few of them. He put napkins, plastic forks, wooden chopsticks and soy sauce packets on the coffee table, along with the take-out containers.

"Do you want a soda?" he asked. "Or some milk?"

"I'll take a soda."

"Wouldn't milk be better for you?"

"Probably, but it sounds icky with Chinese food."

"How about herbal tea instead? That works with chow mein."

She couldn't help but smile. He was being an attentive host. "You don't seem like the herbal tea type."

He smiled, too. "I have my moments."

He certainly did. He got up to brew the tea, and her heart went haywire, kind of like when she'd seen him across the room at the bar.

When he returned with two cups of orange pekoe and a plastic squeeze-bottle of honey, she'd already picked at a portion of her food. He sat on the floor and ate his with chopsticks, which made him seem like a trendy L.A. guy. She wondered if he'd grown up in the city. With Rex, it was difficult to tell.

They finished their lunch in silence. Grateful for the tea, she asked for a second cup. He still had water leftover on the stove, so he poured it for her. She sipped the mild brew, letting it warm her insides. The interview was about to begin.

"How many people know about the baby?" he asked.

"A lot," she admitted. "I told my family and closest friends. The other instructors at my studio know, too, as well as some of the parents and older students. We teach kids and adults." She placed her cup on a napkin. Rex hadn't provided a coaster. "I fainted a few times at work, and that got the gossip mill going. I figured there was no point in denying it." She made a gesture with her hands, creating a pregnant belly. "Eventually I'm going to show."

"How many of them know that a man named Sixkiller is the father?"

"By now? Probably all of them. Why?" She thought about the brown-haired, brown-eyed doll. It certainly looked more like Rex than herself. "Do you think this is racially motivated?"

"It's something to consider, especially since the threat was made while you were in my company, and the doll seemed to favor my genetics."

So he'd noticed, too. Well, of course, he did, she thought. He noticed everything.

He continued. "But I'm not ruling out other scenarios." He handed her a pen and paper. "I'm going to need a list of your family, friends, students, employees, everyone who knows about the baby."

She got offended. "My friends or family would never do this. It has to be a stranger."

"They can't be too much of a stranger if they know that you're pregnant and I'm the father."

Troubled by his logic, she wrote down the names he'd requested, which was a major feat, considering how long the list was. Still, she refused to believe that someone she cared about was out to hurt her. There had to be another explanation.

"Do you have a big family?" he asked.

"Aside from my parents, I have one set of grandparents, some aunts, uncles and cousins."

"Be sure to include them."

"I am." But none of them would ever knife a doll. "We have dinner together every Sunday."

"You'll have to invite me to the next gathering. I assume they're curious about me."

"You assume right." But inviting him to dinner so he could analyze everyone didn't sit well.

He took the completed list. "How does your family feel about the baby?"

"My parents are thrilled about becoming grandparents. Everyone else has been supportive, too."

"They're not concerned or ashamed about you being an unwed mother?"

"Concerned, yes. Ashamed, no. My family isn't judgmental. Well, maybe my great-aunt Annabelle is, but she's almost ninety years old."

"I'm still going to check her out."

"Go ahead." Annabelle could barely get out of her wheelchair, let alone terrorize her pregnant niece.

Rex continued the interview. "Is there anyone who tried to talk you out of having the baby?"

"No."

"What about your girlfriends who were at the bar?"

"They offered to have a baby shower for me when the time comes."

He changed tactics. "Tell me about your old lovers. Former boyfriends, short-lived affairs and other one-night stands."

She took a deep breath. "I've had two serious boyfriends, and no quickie affairs. As for one-nighters, you're it."

"So, you've only been with three men, including me?"

"Yes." Did he consider that unusual for a single woman her age? She wondered how many women he'd been with, but this didn't seem like the time to ask. He was already forming another question for her to answer.

"Did your old boyfriends ever get aggressive with you? Or were they overly possessive during or after your relationship?"

"No. I was with Jamie during high school, but it fizzled out during our college years. The last I heard, he's married with children of his own now."

"And the other boyfriend?"

"Kirk? We dated for two years, but when we moved in together, we realized that we'd made a mistake. It never got bitter, though. We decided that we were better off as friends."

"How friendly are you?"

"Lunch now and then."

"Does he know about the baby?"

She nodded. "But I can't imagine him—"

Rex cut her off. "Write his full name down. Jamie, too. I'm not leaving any stones unturned."

"Are you going to do the same thing with everyone you know? Are you going to investigate your family and friends? Your old lovers?"

"I already told you that I was going to investigate every angle."

But would he be as thorough blaming his side as he would be blaming hers?

"I think you should stay with me until this is over," he said, catching her off guard. "That's what Daniel did when Allie was being stalked."

Although she was curious about the other couple, she didn't want to mimic them. "I can't stay with you."

"Why not?"

Yes, her mind asked—*why not?* He was obviously trying to make good on his promise to protect her.

"Maybe you could stay with me instead." Her home, her pregnant-lady turf, a situation she could control. Or so she hoped.

"I guess I could. I guess it doesn't make a difference which of us goes where."

It mattered to her, and by the time he got to her house, she suspected it would be an issue for him, too.

She couldn't imagine him fitting into her world any more than she could envision fitting into his.

Nonetheless, they agreed to live together, but only until the perpetrator was caught.

Rex carried his bags into Lisa's cottage-style house and got the urge to run. Clean yet cramped, the decor was decidedly feminine. Already he was drowning in floral prints, lace curtains and painted woods. He wished he'd insisted that she stay with him.

"You don't like what I did with it," she said.

Good call, he thought. Regardless, he tried for polite. "It's fine. It's nice. Just point me in the direction of my room."

She led the way instead. He checked her out from behind, then asked himself what the hell he was doing. He'd already planted a life in her womb. He didn't need to create more trouble.

The guest room was small, painted in pastel colors, with a single window that overlooked a thriving vegetable garden.

"Do you rent or own?" he asked.

"I'm a homeowner." A fact of which she seemed proud.

Rex understood. He owned his place, too, and living in Southern California didn't come cheap. They worked hard for what they had.

She gestured to the tight surroundings. "Eventually this is going to be the nursery."

"I'll be sleeping in the baby's room?" He could picture it with a crib and whatnot. The pastel theme would work, too. For a while, anyway. He couldn't imagine a boy standing it for very long.

"Yes, the baby's room." She said it softly.

A moment later, she informed him that her house had been built in the 1940s. He wondered how that was relevant, until she said, "It only has one bathroom."

One head? His place had two full baths, but his condo was only a few years old. "How's the plumbing?"

"It's fine. Unless you flush the toilet while some-one is in the shower. But we won't be doing that."

"I take long showers."

"In the morning or evening?"

"Morning."

"Then we shouldn't have a problem sharing. I bathe at night."

"With bubble bath and scented candles, I'll bet." He suspected that she had fancy bottles every-where.

"Soaking in the tub relaxes me."

"There's nothing wrong with that. It's actually kind of sexy."

"Oh." Lisa angled her head, making her perfectly coiffed bob tilt to one side. "Then thank you, I guess."

"Sure."

Neither of them said anything after that, and the room seemed to shrink even more. He could ac-tually feel them breathing the same air. She was almost close enough to kiss.

But he didn't dare imagine it. His mind was already filled with images of the night he'd stripped her bare.

Apparently so was hers. "Have you been with anyone since you were with me?" she asked, her voice cracking a little.

Rex shook his head. "I don't mess around that much." He glanced at the single bed. He had a king-size at home. "Sometimes I do," he amended. "Sometimes I'm a player."

"I could tell that you were. But I wanted to do something wild that night."

"For your birthday?"

"Yes."

Lisa crossed her arms over her chest, but it didn't strike Rex as a defensive pose. He thought it exhibited a cautious form of shyness.

But she couldn't hide from him. He was right in front of her. Every blood-pumping part of him.

"When I first found out that I was pregnant, I kept debating if I should tell you," she said. "But I figured that when the baby got older, it would ask about its father. And then there I'd be all those years later having to explain."

This way, she'd been honest from the start. He respected that. But it also made him more aware of how emotionally ill-equipped he was to become a parent. He liked being a player.

She dropped her hands and clutched her stomach. "Now all I want is for this baby to be safe."

He was tempted to touch her, to comfort her, but he kept his hands to himself. "I won't let anything happen." Not to her and not to the child she carried. "But you have to cooperate with my investigation."

"I already am. I gave you that list, didn't I?"

Of people she was close to, he thought, some of whom she loved. He knew that couldn't be easy. "I'm sorry about what you've been through today." Was it any wonder her skin was still unnaturally pale?

"I hope I don't have nightmares."

"Maybe you can take something to help you sleep."

"Like those PM pills? I'd have to check with my doctor to see if it's okay. But I'd rather keep drugs out of my system."

"You were right about being a good mom. You're going to do the kid proud."

She loosened the clenching hold on her stomach. "So are you, Rex. Look how protective you are already. Offering to keep us safe."

Because he didn't know how to respond, he said, "I plan on being up late." He gestured to his laptop case. "Running background checks."

"Just with people's names?"

"The system I use only requires first and last names. But it helps to have dates of birth and Social Security numbers, if they're available. I've also got some license plate numbers to check on."

"Yes, I saw you writing them down. Lucky for me my baby's daddy is a P.I."

There she went, complimenting him again.

None of this seemed lucky, but he went ahead and faked a smile. "Oh, sure. You hit the jackpot."

She smiled, too. Only hers seemed genuine. "You even carry a gun."

He nodded, and they both turned serious. A 9mm was clipped to his belt.

"Maybe I should learn to shoot." She'd gone edgy again. A lioness protecting her cub. "You could teach me."

Rex didn't want her jumping the gun, no pun intended. "We'll see, okay? For now, you just need to relax. Panicking won't solve anything."

"I'm not panicking."

Wasn't she? He doubted that she'd ever considered a firearm before. But being put in harm's way changed a person.

"What happened with Daniel and Allie?" she asked suddenly. "Was Allie's stalker caught?"

"Yes, she was."

*"She?"*

"It was a young woman who had schizophrenic delusions about Daniel. She was taken to a psychiatric facility. She wasn't stable enough to stand trial."

"How is that related to the Warrior Society?"

"Daniel recovered a medicine bundle for her family. That's how she knew him, from one of his missions."

Lisa made a thought-provoking face. "Maybe there's a girl out there with delusions about you."

"Maybe, but I doubt it." He'd already explained earlier how the timing was off, how someone associated with him probably wouldn't have known about the baby so soon. Not unless that same someone was connected to Lisa, too. "But I'll check into it."

She searched his gaze, as if looking for answers in his eyes. "Am I going to meet Daniel and Allie? And the close-quarter combat trainer and his pregnant wife?"

"If you want to."

"I do, and your family, too."

"I'm an only child, and my parents live in North Carolina." Eventually he would have to tell them about the baby, but for now, he preferred to keep it to himself. In spite of their own rotten marriage, they would probably bug him about proposing to Lisa and offering their grandchild a legitimate name.

"Is that where you're originally from?"

"Yes. The Qualla Boundary. The Eastern Band Cherokee Indian Reservation," he explained when she gave him a curious look.

"So you're Cherokee?"

"I'm half, from my dad's side. My mom is white." But she was just as traditional as his old man.

"You'll have to teach me about your heritage. For the baby," she added.

"Stuff like that is going to take time." For now,

all he could focus on was who had threatened her. "This case takes priority."

She hiccupped, then tapped her chest, trying to still the jumping motion. "I'm never going to look at dolls in the same way again."

"Someday you might have to. If we have a girl, she'll want to play with them."

"Maybe she'll be a tomboy."

"Are you kidding? A daughter of yours?" He tried to lighten her mood. "Little Miss Sugar and Spice. She's going to be a girlie girl."

Lisa hiccupped again. "I keep seeing it in my head. Its broken body, its chest."

Apparently his teasing hadn't helped. "Try to block the image. Try to clear your mind."

"That's easier said than done." Another hiccup erupted.

"I know. I'm sorry." Was it true that hiccups went away if you scared someone? He wasn't about to try it and find out.

Lisa was already on the verge of nightmares.

## Chapter 3

Lisa made it through the night. No nightmares. But that was because she'd barely slept. You couldn't dream if you were awake.

She curled up in bed, dawn seeping through the sheers. As usual, she was nauseous. Mornings were no longer kind to her.

Fighting her baby-on-board queasiness, she reached for the crackers she kept on the nightstand. She ate slowly, munching on one saltine at a time.

But it didn't help.

She prayed this side effect would go away before too long. Supposedly it would. But she'd heard about women who suffered from morning sickness well beyond their first trimester.

Perish the thought. She would rather die.

No, she thought. Don't think about dying. Or dolls with knives protruding from their fragile little bodies.

Oh, God. She sat up, clutched the water bottle beside her bed and took a cautious sip.

Bad move. The water hit her stomach like a roiling rock. The saltines she'd just eaten weren't going to stay down.

Lisa dashed down the hall to the bathroom. She knelt in front of the commode and lost her cookies or crackers or whatever.

Finally, she made her way to the sink, rinsed her mouth and brushed her teeth. She scrubbed her face and combed her hair, too, trying to feel human again.

Upon exiting the bathroom, her breath caught. There stood Rex, wearing a lightweight T-shirt and drawstring shorts. He was also holding his shaving kit.

"Are you okay?" he asked.

Great. He'd heard her vomit. She hadn't considered her morning sickness when they'd agreed on a bathroom schedule. But she hadn't expected them to wake up at the same exact hour, either. "It's part of the pregnancy."

"Does it happen every morning?"

"Pretty much. But some mornings are worse than others."

"Is it going to happen again? Should I leave the door unlocked?"

Mortified, she blinked at him. She wasn't going to go in there and throw up while he was in the shower. Then again, where else was she going to go? Barfing in a bucket sounded even more disgusting.

"I should be all right." Her empty stomach seemed to be settling. Of course now she was hungry.

"Just in case, I won't lock it." He gestured to the door. "You can come in if you need to."

And risk seeing him in the buff? Lisa sucked in her breath. Not that she hadn't seen his beautifully sculpted body before.

She remembered being sprawled across his lap, watching the tight motion of his abs while he'd lifted her up and down.

"Did you sleep okay?" he asked, jarring her back to the present.

"I tossed and turned, but I made it through." She wanted to move closer to him, but she curbed her desire to breathe him in. "I'll probably take a nap later."

"Is it your day off?"

"Yes. I have classes tomorrow tonight."

"I'd like to go with you tomorrow. As a guest."

"To my studio?" Why? So he could scout for suspects? "I don't think that's a good idea."

"You promised to cooperate, Lisa."

She sighed. Keeping her guard up with him was difficult. He was an aggressive investigator, but he had her best interest at heart. "Okay, but you better not freak everyone out."

"I'm not going to mention the doll. I want to meet everyone first and get a feel for who they are."

"I'm not going to say anything, either." She would have to tell her parents, of course. But she didn't want anyone at the studio to know, not until it was absolutely necessary. "Did you run some background checks last night?"

"Yes, but nothing suspicious surfaced. I've still got plenty of work to do, though."

Because there were lots of people on the list she'd given him. Nervous, she adjusted the bodice of her modest nightgown. "How am I supposed to introduce you?"

"Just use my name."

A simple way of letting everyone know that he was the daddy, she thought. The Sixkiller name had already been bandied about.

She changed the subject. "I'll go start some breakfast. Are pancakes okay?"

"You're going to cook for me? Hell, yes. Pancakes sound great."

"Then I'll see you when you're dressed and ready." Rather than damp and naked, she thought, as she walked away, his handsome image crowding her troubled mind.

After his shower, Rex put on a My Heroes Have Always Killed Cowboys T-shirt and a pair of button-fly jeans, then followed the enticing aroma.

He stood in the doorway of the kitchen and watched Lisa. She'd gotten dressed, as well. She looked soft and pretty in a loose cotton dress and sandals.

She turned and noticed him. She caught sight of the slogan on his shirt, too.

"Your activism is showing," she said.

He shrugged and smiled. "I've got more where this came from."

"I'll bet you do." She motioned to the stove top. "I'm making blueberry pancakes."

"Looks like you're fixing ham and eggs, too."

"I'm famished."

No doubt, he thought. She was eating for two. He still couldn't believe that this was happening, that he was going to have a kid.

"Do you want to eat on the porch?" she asked.

"Sure. Why not?" Since the front door was already open, he glanced in that direction. The porch was rife with potted plants, and amid the greenery was a glass-topped table. "I can put the plates out if you want."

"Thanks. That'd be nice." She showed him where the dishes and flatware were kept.

He scooted past her. "Are we going to sit out there and spy on your neighbors? I can change my shirt if we are. I have one that says Love thy Neighbor, but Don't Get Caught."

She shook her head. "Figures you'd have a shirt like that. Especially with the type of neighbors you have."

"You mean, young and sexy and single?" Rex loved his naughty neighborhood. "What type lives around here? Old and married and crotchety?"

"Nice and normal," she responded, tossing a dish towel at him.

He laughed and tossed it back at her. Were they flirting? Yes, he thought. And he liked it.

Soon they were seated on the porch, a hearty, home-cooked meal in front of them.

Rex decided that he could get used to this. She'd even made cappuccino from one of those commercial-grade espresso machines, decaffeinated for her and the potent stuff for him. He toasted her with his cup. "Here's to vintage suburbia." He glanced around at the other houses, with their colorful flowerbeds and white fences. "Are you sure your neighbors are nice and normal?"

She furrowed her brows. "Why? Do you think you should investigate them?"

"Do they know about the baby?"

"Some of them do."

"Then, yes, I think I should check them out."

"That list of yours keeps getting longer." She rubbed her arms, as if to ward off a sudden chill. "Better to be safe than sorry, right? What would I do without your help? I couldn't handle this on my own."

Her anxious gaze met his, drawing him in, making him even more protective of her.

"I'm going to put my other cases on hold." He needed to devote as much time as he could to this investigation.

"I dread calling my parents." She rubbed her arms again. "They're going to worry something fierce."

And with good reason. Rex was worried, too. What kind of sick bastard maimed a doll and left it in a pregnant woman's car?

"Do you think the police will uncover any evidence?" she asked.

"I don't know." He doubted that fingerprints or DNA had been left behind. Even the knife that had been used seemed generic. It could have come from anyone's kitchen. As for the doll itself, he suspected that tons of stores carried them.

"Maybe I should buy that other car soon."

"The SUV?"

She nodded. "A newer car won't be as easy to break into. And it's safer, with air bags and all of that."

In the silence, she cut into her pancakes. By now, the food on their plates had begun to turn cold. But he was glad that she'd resumed eating. He returned to his meal, too.

After a few more bites, she looked up at him. "Do you think I'm being naive?"

"About what?"

"About who's threatening me? Do you think I should have some sort of feeling about who it could be?"

No way was he going to blame her. "I think you're sweet and trusting. But from now on, you need to be more aware of your surroundings."

"And suspect everyone, the way you do?"

"It's my job to be suspicious."

"Maybe my mommy instincts will kick in, and I'll be able to help you figure out who the bad guy is."

He hoped that her mommy instincts boosted the case. He contemplated touching her stomach, but he feared his hand would tremble. He wasn't ready to meet his kid.

Struggling to regain his composure, he grabbed his cappuccino, taking refuge in the creamy brew.

"Have your friends picked a name?" she asked.

"What?" Her question confused him.

"The couple whose baby is due this month. Have they chosen a name for their daughter?"

"I have no idea."

"You never asked them?"

"No."

"I guess it's too soon for us to discuss names."

For their kid? Way too soon, he thought.

"It helps for me to talk about the baby." Lisa cradled the tummy he'd been afraid to touch. "To think about all the good stuff still to come."

As opposed to the bad stuff that was happening now? "That's understandable."

"I wonder if I'll get cravings."

"Cravings?" he parroted.

"For specific foods."

"Like the pickles-and-ice-cream thing?" That much he knew. That much he'd heard of.

"Yes, but I don't think that's a common craving."

"Then why did it catch on?"

She made a perplexed face, but she was an expressive girl. He figured it was the dance and theater major in her.

"I don't know why it caught on," she said. "Maybe I'll research it online."

"Sounds like a plan." Anything to keep her mind off the danger she was in, he thought, to give her a short reprieve.

And create an illusion of normalcy.


While Lisa napped, Rex worked. He brought his laptop into the living room and ran more background checks. Unfortunately, he came up with nothing. Or at least nothing criminal. Who knew what kind of evil lurked in people's minds?

When Lisa got up, she headed to the bathroom, but she didn't have another bout of sickness. He wasn't deliberately listening for sounds of retching, but he was trying to keep an eye on her.

She came into the living room, and he noticed that her dress was wrinkled. She must have slept in it, making her look soft and rumbled.

"I'm going to fix a snack," she said. "Do you want one?"

"No, thanks." Breakfast hadn't been that long ago.

Soon Lisa returned with a peanut butter sandwich and a tall, frosty glass of milk. He was glad to see that she was getting her calcium. He wondered if she was going to breast-feed, then cursed himself for thinking about it, especially since it made him feel kind of sexual.

Since when did nursing mothers turn him on?

She sat beside him and munched. "How's it going?"

Terrible, he thought. It was all he could do not to look at her breasts. "I did a Google search and discovered that your first boyfriend has a MySpace profile. Mostly it's family stuff. Pictures of his wife and kids. They live in Cincinnati. But that came up in the background check, too."

"Really? I didn't know that he'd moved. I guess that rules him out as a suspect. Ohio isn't exactly around the corner." She took another bite of her sandwich. "What did you find out about Kirk?"

Her second boyfriend, he thought. The one she'd lived with. "I didn't come across anything of interest, other than his financial blog." On the day the doll had been stabbed, Kirk rambled about mutual funds. "His blog gets a lot of traffic."

"He works in the banking industry. But you probably already know that by now."

"Yes, I do." He spent quite a bit of time analyzing Kirk.

"He helped me get the loan on this house."

"Before or after you split up?"

"After."

Rex decided that Kirk required further investigation. You never knew about an old lover, especially when that lover remained active in their ex's life.

"I think I'll go play on the 'Net, too," she said. "Not that you've been playing," she quickly corrected. "But you know what I mean."

Yes, he did. He poked at her ribs. It was as close to her stomach as he'd gotten. "You're going to look up pickles and ice cream?"

She laughed. "And check my e-mails."

"Have fun."

"Loads." She took the half-eaten snack with her.

Less than five minutes later, she screeched, "Rexxx!"

He jumped up and ran into her room. She sat in front of her desktop, as pale as a ghost.

His heart hit his chest. "What happened? What's wrong?"

"I got a creepy e-mail."

He leaned over her shoulder. "What does it say?"

"It's a picture of Alice from *Alice in Wonderland*."

Had he heard her correctly? "Alice?"

"She's swimming in her own tears. See?" She pointed to the image on the screen, a depiction that looked as if it had come from the original storybook. "I was scared of Alice when I was little. She helped me when I got lost, but I didn't trust her."

Rex was baffled. Lisa was talking in riddles, in things that weren't real. "Is that a dream you used to have?"

"No. It happened. I got lost at Disneyland."

Okay, now it was beginning to make sense. Alice was an employee at the Magic Kingdom, walking around in a costume. "Did you get separated from your parents?"

"Yes. I was five years old, and we were in Fantasyland. I was with my mom, waiting in line to order food, and my dad went to find us a table. It was the Fourth of July weekend, so it was packed."

Rex waited for Lisa to continue. He could see the memories in her eyes. But a little girl wouldn't forget the day she'd gotten lost.

"After we got our food, I ran ahead to find Dad. Mom called out to me, but I didn't listen. Then suddenly, I was alone, trapped in scores of people. I was going in the wrong direction and I couldn't find my parents. I just wandered around, crying to myself."

"Is that when Alice found you?"

"No. Maggie and Tim found me. They were strangers at the time. But they became friends with my family after that. They approached Alice, told her that I was lost and asked her what they should do."

"Were you crying when you were with Maggie and Tim?"

"I was crying the entire time. I wasn't supposed to talk to strangers, so I was leery of them. But they turned out to be really nice."

How nice? Rex wondered, his suspicious mind kicking in. "Why were you afraid of Alice?"

"I thought I would fall down the rabbit hole if I got too close to her. But she contacted security and I was taken to the Lost Children Center. Tim and Maggie followed us there. They wanted to be sure that I was reunited with my parents."

"Is your family still friends with Maggie and Tim?"

She nodded, then frowned at him. "You're not planning on putting them on the list, are you?"

"They're fair game, Lisa."

"They're not even in town. They went on a camping trip. My mom is collecting their mail and watering their plants."

"That could be a phony alibi."

"They've been gone for over a week and won't be coming back until sometime next month."

"They're still going on the list." For now, everyone was. He took a closer look at the e-mail. It had been sent from Snow White. Another Disney reference?

"You're not scared of Snow White, too, are you?"

"No. Can you find out who really sent this?"

"I've got a CCFT who can check it out. A certified computer forensics technician," he explained.

"And I'll let Bell know that you got what appears to be another threat." He blew out a breath. "Is there anyone besides your family and Maggie and Tim who knows about the Disneyland incident?"

"Most of my friends know. It's sort of running joke that I'll get lost whenever we go there. But no one has ever been mean about it."

Well, someone was being mean now, preying on childhood fears, reminding Lisa of the tears she'd cried.

"Does Kirk know?"

"Yes, but he never said much about it."

"What about your neighbors?" he asked, trying to narrow down the list.

"Not that I'm aware of." Her voice hitched. "I think I better quit stalling and call my parents. They need to know what's going on."

Rex nodded his agreement. Keeping them in the dark wouldn't do any good.

"They'll probably want to come over." She turned away from the computer to look directly at him. "I'm glad I told you about the baby."

Strangely enough, so was he. Because he was the daddy. Because the tiny heartbeat inside her belonged to him, too.

He left her alone to make her call, and while she was on the phone, he contacted the CCFT.

Something in this case had to give. Something had to shake free.

Before Lisa really did fall down the rabbit hole.

## Chapter 4

Lisa hung up the phone and went in search of Rex. She found him on the porch, only he wasn't sitting at the table. He was perched on the steps.

She got his attention. "My parents are on their way over."

He turned around to look at her. "The CCFT is coming by, too. But it'll be about an hour." He patted the spot next to him. "Join me?"

She sat beside him, and their shoulders brushed. The physical contact made the air in her lungs whoosh out. But every time she got near him, she wanted to move even closer.

"Are you okay?" he asked.

"Right as rain," she responded, trying to keep the conversation light.

He smiled, and the tilt of his lips was slightly crooked and naturally flirtatious. "At least you haven't lost your sense of humor."

Affected by his smile, Lisa exhaled again. What option did she have? Holding her breath and turning blue? "I'm a regular comedienne." She bumped his shoulder and tried for a smile of her own. "Do you like sweets?"

"Why? Are you going to whip up some goodies for me?"

"No, but I'll bet my mom shows up with something. She bakes almost every day. Actually, I bake, too. Mostly when I'm stressed. Sugar is comfort food."

"Then I'd say you're due for some dessert."

"I eat plenty of junk."

"So do I, but then I have to hit the gym even harder." He roamed his gaze over her. "Does dancing keep you thin?"

"I'm sure it helps, but I've never had a weight problem. My parents think I must have inherited a skinny gene."

"From whom?"

"My other parents. The biological ones."

His curious gaze didn't falter. He remained totally focused on her. "Do you know anything about them?"

She shook her head. "It was a closed adoption, so the records are sealed. But it's never mattered to me. My identity doesn't hinge on genetics. I am who I am because of the parents who raised me."

"My identity has always hinged on my heritage."

She studied the rugged angles of his face. He was squinting in the sun, creating tiny lines around his eyes. "The Warrior Society guy?"

"The *mixed-blood* Warrior Society guy. Us half-breeds have more to prove. I think that's why Kyle and I clicked. He walks in both worlds, too."

"Kyle?"

"My friend whose wife is having a baby. He founded our Warrior Society. Joyce was the first white woman he'd ever dated. He used to try too hard to be Indian."

Lisa assumed Joyce was the wife. "Do you date all types?"

He flashed that sexy smile. "Mostly I'm partial to long, lean blondes."

Was that how he viewed her? Although she was tall and trim with wheat-colored hair, she wasn't seductive. She doubted that his other blondes were as homespun as she was. "You're the first guy I've ever dated outside my race. But only because you're the first ethnic guy who asked me out."

His smile went a tad more devilish. "I asked you out?"

Her cheeks turned hot. What he'd done was ask her to bed. "I was trying to be polite."

"I know. I'm just teasing. But maybe I really should take you out sometime."

*Whoosh.* There went the air in her lungs again. "On a real date?"

"Yes, but I'll be a gentleman this time. I won't expect you to go home with me."

Nervous, she reprimanded him. "Like you need to, smarty. You're already living at my house."

"Yeah, in separate bedrooms. What could be more gentlemanly than that?"

Meaning what? That after their date, he wouldn't try to make a move on her? No body-warming hug? No good-night kiss? Relief washed over her, along with a pang of disappointment. Still, she knew it was less complicated to keep things platonic. "You better take me someplace nice."

He chuckled. "What? No Mickey D's or KFC?" Going serious, he shifted his gaze. "Is that your parents?"

She glanced up and saw their car. "Yes, that's them." They were parking in front of the house.

Soon they exited the vehicle. Mom had a worried expression and was carrying a pie. Dad looked just as worried, but he seemed wary, too. His distrustful gaze was fixed on Rex.

Rex stood and offered Lisa a hand. "I think your dad wants to kick my ass."

"Can you blame him? You knocked up his daughter."

"Gee, thanks for reminding me. God, I hope we don't have a girl. If some guy does to her what I did to you, I'd kill him."

Lisa almost laughed. There was an odd sort of irony in all of this. She got a quick chill. Except for the knifed doll and threatening e-mail part. "He isn't as scary as he looks."

"Says who? Daddy's girl?"

Okay, so her father *was* a sight. He stood tall and wide with a big bald head like his favorite "Stone Cold" wrestler. Mom, a full-figured brunette in spring colors, was much gentler, but just as protective. They'd tried for years to have children, but had miscarried every time. To them, Lisa was a blessing, an adoptive miracle, and now that they were retired with plenty of time on their hands, they were anxious to have grandchildren. Lisa's baby was their new everything.

The foursome met on the lawn, and Mom rushed

forward and gave Lisa a maternal hug, pressing the pie pan against her.

Lisa suspected that the men were gazing silently at each other. Rex was still wearing the Killing Cowboys T-shirt. Thank goodness Dad wasn't a country-and-western fan.

Once the introductions were made, Lisa relaxed. Her parents' names were Glenn and Rita, but Rex referred to them as Ma'am and Sir. His military background had become apparent. Or maybe it was his Southern roots. Suddenly he didn't seem like a carefree Californian. He seemed much more proper.

They went inside and talked about the case. Rex didn't hold back. He told her parents that he was going to investigate absolutely everyone in Lisa's life, especially now that the threat had become associated with her childhood.

"Do whatever you have to do." Mom admitted that losing their little girl at the happiest place on earth had been the worst day of their lives. "We couldn't bear to ever lose her again."

Lisa's heart stuck in her throat, and Rex repeated his promise to keep her safe.

That sealed the deal for Dad. He jumped into the discussion, saying to Rex, "When she's not with you, she'll be with us. We'll rearrange our schedules to make sure she's safe."

Lisa listened to them decide her fate. For now, her independence was shot, but she wasn't about to argue. There was more than her well-being at stake. She had a baby to consider. Still, it was tough to imagine having someone with her 24/7. She was used to her freedom.

"Hopefully none of this will be necessary," she interjected. "Not if the computer tech tracks down the person who sent the e-mail."

"You mean, Snow White?" Mom asked, referring to the sender's chosen name. She turned to Rex. "Do you think it's a woman? Or do you think it's a man trying to disguise his gender?"

He responded, "Anything is possible. But as Lisa said, hopefully we're about to find out." He glanced at his watch. "The CCFT should be here soon."

When the technician arrived, Rex escorted him into Lisa's room, with Dad on their heels.

The women stayed out of the way, going into to kitchen to brew a pot of coffee to accompany the pie.

"Rex seems like a good guy," Mom said, looking to her daughter for reassurance that her assumption was right.

Lisa gave her stamp of approval, making the best out of what was happening. "I think he's doing what he can to help me through it." The key lime pie was helping, too. She savored every bite. "He even of-fered to take me on a date."

Mom leaned forward. "So it's getting romantic?"

"No. We're just friends." With flashes of unwel-come heat tossed in, but she kept that bit of infor-mation to herself.

"It's probably better not to jump into anything. You've got enough to deal with. Oh, sweetie, I'm so scared for you."

"I'm scared, too." When the conversation turned to the danger she was in, she wrapped her arms around her stomach, holding on to her baby.

Hours later, the men emerged, and the diagnosis was grim. Lisa didn't understand the technical jar-gon, but she got the gist of it.

Snow White's e-mail was untraceable.

The following day, Rex went to the studio with Lisa. The Heart of Dance was located in a quaint lit-tle shopping center in The Valley and offered in-struction in jazz, hip-hop, tap and ballet.

Rex had already met the students in her adult tap class, and although they'd seemed surprised to see him, they hadn't expressed an unnatural interest in his relationship with Lisa. Sure, they would gossip and make speculations, but none of them stood out in a threatening way.

Of course that didn't absolve them. It just made the investigation more challenging.

After the tap class ended, Rex and Lisa headed to her office. She had clerical work to catch up on, and he was still making his way down the potential suspects list, so they shared her desk, each at their own laptops.

Lisa didn't have another class tonight. She didn't teach as many classes as the other instructors because running the studio was a chore in itself. He admired her work ethic. In that regard, they were cut from the same cloth. He was beginning to think that they actually had something in common.

A knock sounded on the door, and Lisa called out for whomever it was to come in.

A young woman entered. She appeared to be in her midtwenties, with fair skin and short dark hair.

She immediately looked at Rex, then back at Lisa.

"I heard your baby daddy was here," she said, using the trendy reference he'd wondered about. She cast another glance in his direction.

Lisa handled the introduction gracefully. The curious girl was Cathy Leonard, the jazz and hip-hop instructor. Her name was on the list, but he hadn't run a background check on her yet.

Rex said hello and shook her hand. She had a firm grip and a bright smile.

"You're the talk of the studio," she told him. "Everyone has been saying how handsome you are." Then to Lisa in a mock whisper, "He's totally gorgeous."

Rex bit back a grin. Lisa was blushing.

Still, she managed a response, acknowledging his supposed appeal. "That's why I'm having a baby with him."

"No doubt." Cathy bounced on the balls of her feet. "I just love babies."

Rex's sense of humor vanished. She loved cuddling them? Or stabbing them?

Cathy was the first person at the studio to actually seek him out, to insinuate herself into the situation.

He took a closer look at her: the fair skin, the dark hair, the pretty perfection.

Like Snow White.

Damn, Rex thought. *Damn.* She really did look like the fairy-tale character. She even had a red headband in the front of her hair. All she needed to complete the package was a blue-and-yellow dress. He knew all about Snow White's wardrobe because he'd researched her online.

Regardless, Cathy's outfit was similar to Lisa's. Both sported black dance pants and white T-shirts with The Heart of Dance logo.

So what was the deal with Miss Red Headband? Rex intended to find out. He asked, "How long have you worked here?"

"A little over a year." She kept smiling. "How long have you been a P.I.?"

His radar went up even more. "You know what I do?"

"Sure. Everyone does. Gossip, you know. I love those old gumshoe movies. You have a cool job."

She loved babies. She loved private eyes. And she resembled Snow White. Was she the perpetrator? Or an innocent coincidence?

He answered her original question. "I've been a P.I. for thirteen years."

"You must be good."

Was she baiting him? "I am."

"I'll bet Lisa thinks so." She winked at her boss, making her double entendre clear.

Was this girl for real?

A short silence ensued, but she didn't seem to mind. She remained as upbeat as ever.

"I have a great guy myself," she said.

"Do you?" Rex was all ears. "And what does he do?"

"Nelson? He's a computer systems analyst."

Another coincidence? Or another obvious clue?

He glanced at Lisa. She hadn't been alarmed until now. Her chest rose and fell with her next breath.

"Nelson what?" he asked, inquiring about a last name.

"Clemmons. Nelson Clyde Clemmons. Isn't that a great handle?" This time, she rocked on her heels. "Hey, here's an idea. Do you guys want to have dinner with us tomorrow? We could go to a nice restaurant."

"Sure, we could do that," Rex responded.

"Cool. Nelson keeps saying that we should have more couple friends. I'm sure he'll want to go out."

Cathy bebopped again. She was like Snow White on speed. She had way too much energy.

As for Lisa, she just sat there, letting Rex handle the conversation. But he suspected that she was going to rip into him about dinner after Cathy left.

As if on cue, the other woman glanced at the clock on the wall. "Yikes! I better go. I have a class to teach." She smiled at both Rex and Lisa. Then to her boss, she said, "I'll call you later and we can figure out a time."

She darted out the door, closing it behind her.

Lisa rounded on Rex. "Why did you accept that invitation? What if she's the one? I completely forgot that her boyfriend worked with computers until she mentioned it. He could have sent the e-mail for her."

"That's exactly why I accepted the invitation. I want to pick their brains. Maybe even bring them into the fold and ask for their help."

"You mean, tell them that I'm being threatened?"

"If they're the perpetrators, they might trip up and reveal something they shouldn't." He poured her a cup of water from the cooler in the corner. She looked as if she could use the refreshment.

She accepted the cup. "This is crazy."

"What is?"

"Making Cathy out to be a criminal. She's quirky, but she's never been anything but sweet to me." Lisa drank the water. "In fact, aside from her boyfriend's job, there's no reason for me to suspect her. I must be getting paranoid."

"She looks like Snow White."

Lisa gaped at him. "What are you talking about?"

"The dark hair, the light skin, the cutesy headband."

"Oh, my goodness. I guess she kind of does."

"I'll bet at one time or another she's been Snow White for Halloween."

"I don't know about that. Last year we all dressed up, and she was a frog. She picked that costume because she's always bouncing around."

"Yeah, I noticed how much energy she has."

"I can't imagine her stabbing a doll."

"She was off that day."

"The studio is closed on Mondays. Everyone was off."

"I know, but I need to find out if she has an alibi. Just bear with me on going out to dinner with them."

"All right. But tell me this…if she is the perpetrator, then what's her motive? Why would she threaten our baby? And why would she get her boyfriend involved?"

"I'm still working on that part." But he hoped that by tomorrow night, he would be closer to figuring it out.

# Chapter 5

After work, Lisa decided to bake cookies. Yesterday she'd sent the rest of the pie back home with her mom when she should have kept it. Today of all days, she was in need of comfort food.

She was overwhelmed, in more ways than one. Besides agreeing to go out with Cathy and Nelson, the very people who might be threatening her, she was also troubled by what Cathy had said. The other woman had called her and Rex a couple.

She frowned at the bowl in front of her. Why did that matter? Did she want to be a couple with him?

She glanced his way. He was standing next to her, watching her play Betty Crocker.

When he reached into the bowl and snagged a glob of the dough with a big wooden spoon he'd taken off the counter, she smacked his hand.

He chuckled, ate what he'd stolen and went after another spoonful.

"Cut it out, Rex."

"Come on, be a sport. Do you know how long it's been since I've had cookie dough?" He answered his own question. "Since I was a kid living at home."

She moved the bowl away from him. She'd just added the chocolate chips. "You're not a kid anymore. If you want those types of privileges, go find yourself a wife."

"Oh, sure. And what do I tell her? 'Oh, by the way, I'm having a baby with this hot little mama.'"

What a con. "I hate it when you flirt with me."

"No, you don't. You like it. I can tell." He went ahead and flirted some more. "And you like being a mama, too. You've got that glow they talk about." He leaned into her, maneuvering his way back to the bowl. "You're beautiful, Lisa. Motherhood looks good on you."

Damn him, she thought. Did he have say all the right things? He was close enough to nuzzle her neck. She could feel him breathing against her skin.

He reached around and made another play for the

unbaked treat, returning to their "wife" conversation. "Just so you know, I'm never getting married."

"Never?" She turned to face him. "Ever?"

"Nope." He put down the spoon. "I'd make a terrible husband."

"That's what you said about being a dad."

"I said that I wouldn't make a very good dad. That's not the same as terrible."

"You were wrong about the dad thing. I think you're going to do just fine."

"Maybe." He reached out, and his hand hovered over her stomach, as if he meant to touch her. "But I'm still scared."

She appreciated his honesty. "So am I. But most first-time parents probably are." She looked into his eyes—those overly dark eyes. "You might change your mind about being a husband someday."

"Not a chance." He dropped his hand without touching her. "My parents set a rotten example, snapping at each other all the time. Just the thought of marriage leaves a bitter taste in my mouth."

Lisa couldn't deny her dreams. Like most girls, she wanted the prospect of forever, but only with the right guy. And Rex wasn't him, she reminded herself. "Have you ever been in a serious relationship?"

He shook his head. "I've never even come close to commitment." He scoffed at his bachelorhood, but he did it jokingly and with one of his sexy smiles. "Maybe if my lovers were as handy in the kitchen as you are."

"You would have reconsidered?" Her heart was doing little swan dives, and she could have kicked herself for it. "Sooo…" She dragged out the word. "Just how many women have you been with?"

His smile faded. "Are you asking me that because you're curious or because I promised to investigate my old lovers for the case?"

"Both," she responded, even if, at the moment, curiosity won out.

"Truthfully, I'd rather not spout off a number."

"Do you even know the number?" She couldn't keep from challenging him, especially after all of the personal stuff she'd divulged.

"Of course I do. I mess around, but I'm not irresponsible. Not in this day and age. I practice safe sex, and I keep names and contact information."

She'd had to kiss and tell, but he wouldn't? Talk about a double standard. To chide him, she pointed to her to tummy and said, "You botched the safe-sex part."

"That wasn't my fault. That was—"

"What?" she pressed.

He dragged a hand through his thick, dark hair, messing it up and making the strands spike. "Just something the Creator wanted to happen, I guess."

Unsure of what to say, she finished readying the cookies for the oven.

"Why are you angry with me?" he asked.

She turned, met his gaze and felt her heart do another of those annoying dives. "I'm not."

"Sure seems like it."

"I'm just edgy." And fighting an attraction to him that she wished would go away. As the father of her child, he was going to be part of her life for a very long time.

Too long, she thought.

To curb her emotions, she said, "I plan on getting married someday, and then you won't be this baby's only father."

"Don't throw some guy in my face who doesn't exist yet. I'm the daddy. Me. Not some stranger."

He sounded jealous, which gave her a strange sense of satisfaction. She softened her tone. "Kids can have more than one set of parents."

"Says the adopted girl who isn't interested in the parents who conceived her?"

"That has nothing to do with our child."

"Sure it does. Your genetic history will be part of the baby's history, too."

"I've survived just fine without knowledge of my genetics. Besides, I already told you, it was a closed adoption. I'm not going to go poking around, looking for sealed documents."

"If you ever change your mind, I can get past the closed part. I've done adoption searches before."

She gaped at him, then snapped her mouth shut. He was a P.I. after all. "Just concentrate on who's threatening me, okay?"

"I am." He stepped forward and skimmed his knuckles along her jaw. "All I think about is keeping you safe."

Mercy, she thought. He was saying all the right things again. And his touch, oh, his touch. She shivered like the smitten girl she was, recalling the wicked warmth he'd incited on the night they'd made the baby.

"Don't do this, Rex."

"Do what?"

"Make me feel things I shouldn't feel."

Realization dawned instantly in his eyes. "I didn't mean to." He took his hand away. "I was only trying to comfort you. Damn, this gets confusing."

She knew he meant the attraction that seesawed between them. "I try not to think about it, but sometimes it creeps in."

"That happens to me, too," he responded.

"So keeping me safe isn't *all* you think about?"

"No, but I'm only human." Before things got too

awkward, he saved the moment, cracking a silly joke. "Maybe we should jump each other's bones again, only really badly this time."

"That's not funny." But she laughed anyway. "With our luck, it would be even better."

"Yeah. Then we'd never get over it. We'd be old and gray and reminiscing about all the hot stuff we did."

"No kidding." Repeating it would be a mistake. Exciting, but dangerous. She banished the thought.

Once was more than enough.

While Lisa put the cookies in the oven, Rex took out the trash. No, that wasn't completely true. He'd gone outside to get some air, too.

The conversation he'd had with Lisa only made him want her more. But rekindling their one-nighter wasn't his agenda. He was here to catch the perpetrator and be on his merry way.

What merry way? They were having a baby. He couldn't go skipping off forever. Regardless, they had to set boundaries, lines that shouldn't be crossed.

So why did he want to say "To hell with it" and haul her off to bed? Simple answer: Because he was using the body part below his belt instead of his brain.

He pushed those thoughts aside and returned to

the kitchen to discuss Cathy and Nelson. He needed to stay focused on the case.

Lisa was wiping down the counters. He stood in the doorway and watched her. To him, she looked vulnerable, with her hair tucked behind her ears and flour dusting her blouse.

"I'll be with you the entire time tomorrow," he said, moving farther into the room. "I won't leave your side."

She looked up at him. "It's going to be strange having dinner with them, wondering if they're guilty." She rinsed the dish cloth. "I'm glad that you're going to stay close to me."

"Always," he told her, even if *always* only meant until the case was solved. After that, their time together would be based on the baby's needs.

She resumed cleaning the kitchen, and he asked, "Can I do anything to help?"

"Thanks, but I'm just about done." She stopped, smiled. "Here." She extended the bowl to him. "You can have what's left of the batter."

Rex accepted the offering and scraped the bowl with the same wooden spoon as before, eating the sticky substance from it.

She looked at him and laughed. "The big bad warrior."

"Yeah, don't tell anyone. Damn, this is good." He held out the spoon. "Want some?"

She came forward, and he fed her a bite. By the time he realized how intimate it was, it was too late. While she licked the spoon, their gazes locked.

A jolt of sexual energy blasted down his body, igniting the metal teeth on his zipper and making the rebellious body part strain against it.

Lisa stepped back and dabbed her mouth. He wanted to kiss her senseless.

"I should check on the cookies." She fumbled with the oven door. Clearly, she was feeling the attraction, too.

Apparently their little talk earlier hadn't made a dent in either of their libidos.

"They're not quite done," she said.

He could have told her that. The timer she'd set hadn't gone off yet.

"I'll rinse the bowl." He went to the sink and doused it, struggling to drown his hormones, as well. He opened the dishwasher and tried to make room, but couldn't get the bowl to fit.

"I'll do it." She attempted to take over, and the tips of their fingers connected.

It could have been the tips of their tongues. Blood pulsed through Rex's veins. His heart raced, too. The big bad warrior couldn't get his vitals under control.

"I'll hand wash the bowl," Lisa said, giving up on finding a place for it in the dishwasher. By now, she seemed jittery. She was in as bad as shape as he was.

But she managed to fill the sink with sudsy water. He should have left the kitchen, but he stayed, wanting to be near her.

When the oven timer finally sounded, she busied herself with the cookies again. He waited around for them to cool, using it as an excuse to torture himself.

"I'll get the milk." He proceeded to pour two frosty glasses.

She put the cookies on a plate, and they sat at the table and made pigs of themselves. But stuffing their faces didn't help. The warm, gooey sweetness made him want her even more. He thought about sitophila or whatever it was called. From what he knew, it was the desire to eat foods off the body of another person. Something he hadn't craved until now.

Rex had never been the fetish type, but being around Lisa was doing kinky things to him.

Was she a siren in disguise?

Right. A pregnant siren. A suburban seductress who owned a cute little dance studio and baked cookies.

"I'm full," she said.

"Me, too." Full of sexual insanity. "No more for me."

"Me, neither." She cleared the table, domestic as ever. "It's getting late. I think I'll go soak in the tub."

He cursed in his mind. Now he had to envision her gloriously naked and surrounded by scented bubbles.

Would the madness ever end?

He tried to block the image. "I should get back to work."

"And see what you can find on Cathy and Nelson?"

Rex nodded. Lisa had given him Cathy's Social Security number and birth date from her employee file, which would help him run a thorough search. "I'll probably be up late."

"Not me. I'm beat. After my bath, I'm going to turn in."

"Sure. Okay. Sleep tight." He watched her walk away, torn between the need to keep her safe and just plain keep her.

Rex worked for hours, but he didn't uncover any disturbing information. Cathy Leonard and Nelson Clemmons appeared to be responsible citizens.

Cathy's Social Security number revealed a good credit score and no aliases. Neither she nor Nelson had a criminal record. They didn't hail from violent families. Cathy had gotten a few parking tickets, and Nelson had been popped for jaywalking, but the fines had been paid on time. Both had been born and raised in Southern California, living with their parents until they'd moved in with each other. Nelson had a degree from a technical college; Cathy was well schooled in dance.

Of course he was going to have to dig deeper for warped religious affiliations, racial bigotry, a personal vendetta or anything else that might motivate them to threaten Lisa and the baby.

He kept searching, although he doubted that he would find much more about them online. His job entailed footwork, too. Hopefully the dinner tomorrow night would reveal the things he was looking for.

If not, he would continue his quest until he cleared them as suspects or proved that they were the perpetrators.

His cell phone rang, and he checked the display screen and discovered that it was his mom. She was calling late. North Carolina was three hours ahead, but she'd always been a bit of a night owl.

He stalled, debating if he should answer it. She had the annoying habit of sticking her nose into his life, and he wasn't in the mood for twenty questions. Then again, if he didn't pick up, she would only call back until she got him.

Marie Sixkiller was a persistent woman.

"Hi, Mom," he said, instead of the customary "Hello."

"I was beginning to think you were avoiding me."

"I thought about it."

She chided him right back. "How L.A. of you."

He smiled, picturing her in the modest house where he'd grown up. She would be seated on their outdated sofa—the one his dad had reupholstered years ago—and wearing an old robe and fuzzy socks. Her hair wouldn't be in curlers, though. At least she didn't take her dowdy image that far.

"When are you going to visit?" she asked. "We miss you."

"I don't know. For now, I'm swamped."

She exhaled a big, noisy sigh. She was a Southern Baptist with a knack for drama. "You should at least come for the fair. That will give you some time to plan the trip."

He had to admit that the Cherokee Indian Fair was his favorite event, during his favorite time of year. He loved the crisp fall weather, the carnival, the fireworks, the music, the traditional food and arts and crafts.

"Maybe," he said.

"Oh, Rex, you're always so vague."

"I have a lot going on."

"Like what?"

A woman and unborn child to protect, he thought. "Nothing that concerns you." Yeah, right. Only her grandbaby.

"You're as tight-lipped as your dad."

"Is he asleep?"

"Snoring, as usual."

Such an unhappy pair, Rex thought. Was it any wonder he was keeping Lisa and their kid to himself? Nonetheless, he got a pang of homesickness, and he imagined bringing them to the fair.

Was that even possible? The fair was in October. The little one probably wouldn't even be born yet. Some expectant father he was. He didn't know Lisa's due date.

"I should go, Mom."

"Go where?"

"Just go. I have things to do."

"I love you, son," she said, making his heart ache.

"I love you, too. And Dad," he added.

They said goodbye, and when he hung up, he was tempted to check on Lisa, curious if she cradled her stomach while she slept.

But he steered clear of her room and the conflicting emotion that went with it.

# Chapter 6

The next night's dinner was at a steak and seafood place. Cathy and Nelson had let Rex and Lisa choose the location, and Rex had suggested this restaurant because it was dimly lit and traditional. He hoped that the atmosphere would create a relaxed vibe.

Lord knew they needed it.

Inside the booth, Cathy chattered incessantly, and Nelson was overly quiet. Lisa picked at her meal, quiet, as well. Rex did his best to make the situation seem normal. He hadn't mentioned the case yet.

Nelson kept glancing at Lisa. He was tall but slightly built, with light brown hair and what most people would consider average features. In a lineup, he wouldn't stand out.

Although the looks he was giving Lisa didn't strike Rex as amorous, he wondered if the other man had a hidden crush on her. That would provide motive.

And what about Cathy? Was she involved? Or had Nelson stabbed the doll and used Snow White in the e-mail to cast blame on his girlfriend? If cornered, would he claim that she was as computer savvy as he was?

Rex's mind cluttered with even more questions.

Had Nelson been stalking Lisa? Watching her from afar? Had he collected information about Lisa from Cathy? The brunette yapped about anything and everything.

At the moment, she was talking about Barker, her beloved new puppy, a Chihuahua/poodle mix or Chipoo, if you will.

"He loves playing at the beach," she said. "He's just the cutest little thing. Lisa, would it be all right if I brought him to studio so everyone can see him?"

Lisa nodded, and Cathy clapped her hands like a kid. Nelson frowned at his jumbo shrimp.

Finally he said to Lisa, "Are you all right? You don't seem well."

She looked up at him, then over at Rex, who sat next to her. He'd promised to stay close, and he was. But clearly she didn't know how to respond to Nelson. This dinner was taking its toll on her.

Rex gave her an out. "If you're not feeling well, we can go."

"No, it's okay." Apparently she was willing to stick it out for the investigation. "Sometimes I get a little tired from the pregnancy." She lifted her fork in a show of steak-and-mushroom support. "But the food is good."

Below the table, Rex put his hand on her thigh, letting her know what was about to happen. He figured this was a good time to get the ball rolling, especially now that Chatty Cathy was quiet, too.

Rex said, "There's another reason Lisa isn't doing well. Someone has been threatening her and the baby."

Cathy gasped and said, "What?" and Nelson leaned forward, exhibiting what appeared to be a concerned gaze. He was either a genuinely nice guy or a psychopath in sheep's clothing.

Rex explained, leaving out a few pertinent details about the doll. He did the same thing with the e-mail. If Cathy or Nelson accidentally mentioned any of his omissions, their guilt would be clear.

"I'm so sorry," Cathy said to her boss. "How could someone do that to you? And why?"

"I don't know, but Rex is trying to find out."

"I'm never going to be Snow White for Halloween again." Cathy gave a shudder. "She was my standby costume when I couldn't think of anything else to be."

Lisa glanced at Rex, silently acknowledging that he'd been right about the other woman dressing up as Snow White. Rex wished that she wouldn't have glanced his way, but it was too late do anything about it. Nelson caught the look and zeroed in on the truth.

"Do you suspect us?" he asked.

Before Rex could respond, Cathy shoved at her boyfriend's shoulder. "Oh, my God. That's an awful thing to say. Why would they think we did it?"

"Because I'm a computer systems analyst and you resemble Snow White."

"That's true." Rex spoke honestly, taking a different route than he'd originally planned. Nelson was too astute to fool. "You did cross our minds."

The other man blew out a tight breath. "Well, it wasn't us."

"Maybe it was just you or just her."

"It wasn't." Nelson got defensive, a natural reaction for someone being accused of something he claimed he didn't do.

"Then provide some alibis, and I'll check them out."

"Fine. We'll tell you whatever you want to know."

"Yes, we will." Cathy looked mortally wounded by what was taking place. If her story checked out, Rex would apologize. Lisa already looked ready to apologize. She was staring morosely at her plate.

At this point, Rex didn't know what to think. "Where were you last Monday, between 1:00 p.m. and 2:00 p.m.?" The hour in which Lisa had been in his office and the doll had been left in her car.

"I was on a plane," Nelson said quickly. "Returning from Las Vegas. I attended a software conference that weekend."

His alibi would be easy enough to check. "And you?" Rex asked Cathy.

She got flustered. She wasn't sure where she'd been until she checked her electronic day planner. Then she said, "I took the puppy to get his second set of shots."

"At what time?"

"Ten o'clock."

"What about after that?"

"I went to the Glendale Galleria to shop. I took Barker with me. In one of those little doggie purses."

"Did you buy anything?"

"No, but I was there for hours. I had lunch at the Mexican place in the food court. That's probably where I was between one and two."

Probably wasn't good enough. Rex would be headed to the mall tomorrow.

"Satisfied?" Nelson asked.

Not particularly, Rex thought.

Nelson got up and grabbed his girlfriend's hand. They hadn't finished their meals, but they were leaving.

"Don't expect Cathy back at work," he told Lisa.

After they were gone, Lisa looked at Rex, her eyes clouding with tears.

"We should go, too," she said, pushing her half-eaten steak aside.

He nodded. She was wrung out, tired and confused. She looked as if she needed some sleep.

Lisa couldn't sleep. At half past twelve, she climbed out of bed and headed to the kitchen for a cup of warm milk. All she wanted was for this case to get solved. All she wanted was her old life back.

As if that were possible. Feet bare, she padded down the narrow hallway. Her life was changed forever. The baby, Rex…

*Rex.* His name brought her up short. There he was, working on his laptop, the glow from the screen casting shadows on his strong-boned face. Next to him was a bottle of beer.

Lisa suspected that he preferred the living room

to the guest room because small spaces made him feel boxed in. She on the other hand liked to be cocooned. Held close, kept warm.

Not a good thing to think about right now.

She considered going back from whence she came, but he sensed her presence. Like a lone wolf, he lifted his head, nostrils flared.

Too late to flee.

The ritual began. His eyes on her; her eyes on him.

She imagined that she looked vulnerable in a blush pink, ruffle-hemmed nightgown, with her hair swept away into a barely there ponytail, too-short tendrils framing her cheeks.

"I couldn't sleep," she said, cutting into the quiet.

His gaze was still riveted to hers. "Me, neither."

She tried to glance away, but she couldn't seem to break the connection. He lifted his beer and took a swig, wetting his mouth.

She hoped her nipples didn't harden. When the moon slipped past the window, she wondered if it was making her gown transparent, if he could see the outline of her breasts, her panties, her entire body.

No, she thought. The material was heavy enough to deflect moonlight.

But still…

The memory of being naked in his arms was almost more than she could bear. To combat the feeling, she told her herself to pass "Go" and head directly to the kitchen.

But she stopped when he said, "I'm sorry about what happened at the restaurant. It wasn't supposed to turn out like that."

He'd already apologized earlier, but she appreciated that he cared enough to mention it again.

"This is going to sound awful," she told him. "But there's a part of me that hopes their alibis don't check out and you uncover some evidence against them. But only because I want the horror to end." A lump of shame clogged her throat. "How unfair is that to them if they're innocent?"

He closed his laptop, and the glow around his face disappeared. He was in the dark, except for the moonlight she'd worried about.

"It's okay to feel that way, Lisa. It's okay to want it to be over." He spoke quietly, indicative of his mood. "I'll get started on their alibis tomorrow. Your parents can come over while I'm gone."

"I have to work."

"Then they can go to work with you."

"I'll have to teach Cathy's classes until I find someone to replace her."

"If I clear her, maybe she'll come back."

"And maybe she'll be mad at me forever."

"She seemed more hurt than angry. But who the hell knows? It could've been an act. I'm usually good at judging people, but this case is different."

Because it was personal, she thought. Because he was so close to it.

While he pulled on the beer again, she got another of those girl-to-guy pulses. He looked rough and tumbled and wildly protective of her. It made her want him.

"I never got my milk," she said.

"I'm sorry. What?"

"I came out here for warm milk."

"Then you should go get it."

Yes, she should. She made a beeline for the kitchen.

Alone at last, she went to the fridge, then the stove, where she heated the milk in a pan.

Soon she heard footsteps. Apparently he'd decided to follow her. The light above the stove shone softly, and the flame on the gas burner flickered.

Another intimate setting, she thought. She couldn't escape it.

"I guess we might as well get used to these hours," he said. "With midnight feedings and all that."

He was talking about the baby. "We? You won't be staying here by then." She watched the pan, making sure the milk didn't boil. Or was she watching it to avoid eye contact with him? "Not unless the threats are still going on."

"They won't be. I swear, they won't."

They went silent, until he motioned to the stove and said, "I've never had warm milk."

"Do you want to try it?"

He lifted his beer. "Thanks, but I've got my drink."

"Oh, of course." He wasn't about to mix the two. She went back to watching the pan.

"Wouldn't it have been easier to heat it in the microwave?"

She shook her head. She was still avoiding direct eye contact, catching only peripheral views. "It gets hot spots. So do baby bottles, or so I've heard. But I think I'm going to…" When she realized what she was about to say, she let her words drift.

He picked up where she left off. "Breast-feed? I wondered if you were going to do that."

She chanced a glance. "You did?"

"Yes, but it was just clinical curiosity."

Who was he trying to kid? Breast-feeding had struck him in a sexual way otherwise he wouldn't have been compelled to mention it. "You're a terrible liar, Rex."

He scrunched up his face. "So shoot me for being a guy." He gentled his expression. "I can't help it if I think it's a sensual image. You keep making me feel things I don't normally feel. Even those warm, gooey cookies did a number on me."

She wasn't about to ask him what he meant. Warm and gooey sounded bad enough. She turned away. "My milk is done." Even it hadn't been, she would have used it as an excuse.

His voice sounded behind her. "Are you going to take it back to your room?"

"Yes."

"Want me to tuck you in?"

Good grief. She spun around to tell him to knock off the twisted humor, but she could see that he was serious.

She sucked in her breath. "I don't think that's a very good idea."

"I won't try anything."

Heaven help her, but she wished that he would. "When's the last time you tucked a woman into bed without joining her?"

"Never." He smiled like the modern rogue that he was. "But there's always a first." He finished his beer and discarded the empty bottle. "I'll just pretend that you're out to here now." He looped his hands over his abs-of-perfection stomach. "That'll cure me."

"Gee, thanks."

"Sorry, but it's the only fantasy about you I haven't had yet."

"Then I don't have much to worry about, do I? I'll have a swollen belly soon enough."

"Let me tuck you in, Lisa. Let me sit with you until you finish your milk."

How could she refuse? He was the father of her child and the investigator struggling to stop the threats. Rex Sixkiller was the most important man in her life right now.

They walked to her room, and she warned herself to not feel too much. Since her bed was unmade, there wasn't much for him to do by way of tucking her in.

She climbed under the covers and leaned against the headboard, and he handed her the milk. She wrapped all ten fingers around the cup, taking solace from its warmth.

Rex scooted in beside her, but he sat on top of the blanket, creating a fluffy barrier between them. He, too, leaned against the headboard.

"It's shiny in here at night," he said.

Lisa glanced around, trying to see her room through his eyes. A golden-hued Tiffany-style lamp was on, showcasing eyelet sheers, a lace valance and a stenciled border. An iridescent vase with fresh flowers decorated an antique chest of drawers, along with partially melted candles and a shimmering display of glass fairies, which she'd been collecting for years.

She defended her feminine side. "It's my sanctuary."

"It's pretty." He turned to look at her. "Just like you."

The milk she'd just sipped heated her from the inside out. Or was it him? "Thank you."

He smiled. "You're welcome."

Yes, it was definitely him.

His smile shifted to a grin. "It's naughty, too."

She rolled her eyes. There he went, flirting, teasing her, being his usual self. "It is not."

"Are you kidding? It's a den of debauchery. All those half-naked fairies." He pointed to the figurines. "Pure sin."

"Better than you and all those *Playboy*s."

He chuckled. "You got me there."

"I wish I didn't like you so much," she said.

"Because I read *Playboy?*"

Because she was going to miss him when they were no longer living under the same roof. "Because you're growing on me."

"More like inside you. You've got Cherokee blood in there."

Yes, their baby. Suddenly fear coiled itself around her tummy. She put her milk down. "What if something happens and I lose it? What if—"

"Don't say that. Don't even think it." He angled

his body more toward hers. "I'll ask the Creator to talk to the Little People. They've been known to protect children."

"What Little People?"

"Ancient Cherokees believed in fairies. In our folklore, they're called *Yunwi Tsundi* or Little People. I suppose they're more like dwarfs than the fairies you collect, but they're just as magical. They love music, and they spend half of their time drumming and singing."

"What do they look like?"

"They're small, of course, and just as attractive as your fairies. Their hair flows almost to the ground."

She realized that she'd just gotten her first Cherokee lesson from him. "Maybe I should start collecting Little People figurines, too."

"I'm not sure where you'd find them. Besides, they're immortals, so they'd probably disappear."

Touched by his sense of magic, she liked him even more. "It seems like I've known you for longer than four days."

"If you include the night we hooked up and that terrible morning after, it totals six days."

"It wasn't that terrible."

"Yes, it was. You could barely look at me."

She was looking at him now. "So I got a little shy. I'm a good girl."

"Tell me about it. I knew from the moment I first saw you that you were the wholesome type."

"Then why did you pursue me?"

He gave her a playful nudge. "Because I'd always heard that good girls are bad girls who don't get caught."

Lisa nudged him right back. "Well, you heard wrong."

"Why? Because you got caught?"

By *caught,* she assumed he meant pregnant. "That's one way of putting it."

"Yeah, we're quite a pair." He quit goofing around. "Are you ready to get some sleep?"

"I'm ready to try."

"Then hand me your cup, and I'll turn out the light and leave you alone."

She wanted to ask him to stay, but she wasn't that courageous. Or that crazy. "Thanks, Rex."

"Sure." He didn't touch her, but he looked as if he wanted to skim her cheek or maybe even kiss her forehead.

As requested, she gave him her cup so he could take it into the kitchen, and when he turned out the light, she closed her eyes.

Anxious for morning to come, simply so she could see him again.

## Chapter 7

Lisa awakened to the aroma of breakfast. Rex was cooking? No, that didn't seem likely. Maybe he'd gone out and gotten some home-style takeout. Whatever it was, it smelled heavenly.

Eager to see him, she jumped out of bed, and got an instant punch of queasiness. Damn. She sat back down and reached for the ever-present crackers.

*Nibble. Nibble.* Crumbs dropped onto her lap.

A knock sounded on the door.

Shoot. She didn't want Rex to see her like this. She wanted to make a pretty impression. She wanted to sweep into the kitchen and make him smile.

A woman's voice called out from the other side. "Lisa?"

"Mom?"

"Yes, it's me. May I come in?"

"Okay." At least with her mom, she didn't have to worry about being sick or even looking sick. Not that it should matter with Rex, either. But it did.

She couldn't help the way she was starting to feel about him. They were becoming close, much too close.

The door opened, and Rita Gordon entered. As always, she was warm, loving and sympathetic.

"Oh, honey," she said. "Can I get you anything?"

Rex, Lisa thought. She wanted Rex. Now she didn't care if he saw her this way. She'd been queasy in front of him before. "I'll be all right. Nothing a few saltines won't cure."

"You're not going to throw up?"

She shook her head. It was actually starting to subside. She'd gotten lucky today.

Mom sat next to her on the bed. She was wearing one of her pretty spring ensembles, but her hair wasn't as coiffed as it usually was, indicating that she'd been in a bit of a rush when she'd gotten ready.

"Rex called and asked your dad and me to come over."

That explained her hastily done hair. "Where is he?"

"Your dad? He's waiting to eat his share of the breakfast I cooked. Biscuits and gravy."

Lisa hadn't been asking about her dad. She wanted to know about the father of her child. The man driving her to distraction. "What about Rex?"

"He left when we got here. He wanted to get an early start on checking those alibis. He told us about Cathy and Nelson. Can you imagine if it's them? Cathy always seemed so sweet."

"That's what I told Rex."

Mom continued, "He spoke to the police this morning."

"He did?" Lisa's pulse spiked. "Do they have any leads?"

"No. There's nothing, honey. Nothing at all."

"So it's up to Rex." Her one-night knight. She glanced wistfully at the fairies, replacing them in her mind with Cherokee Little People.

"So it seems." A pause, then, "You're not falling for him, are you?"

Yikes. She turned away from the figurines to look at her mom, who was wrinkling her forehead. "No, of course not. I already told you it wasn't romantic."

The older, wiser woman wasn't buying it. "He's

got an irresistible formula. Rough. Handsome. Protective. Who wouldn't fall for that?"

Although Lisa's morning sickness was gone, her anxiety wasn't. "We haven't been together since that first night."

"Yes, but how long are you going to be able to resist him? With him living at your house, you need to be careful."

Shielding her emotions, Lisa went flippant. "What's the point? I'm already pregnant."

"I meant careful in here." Mom tapped her own heart, making a thumping motion with her hand.

The advice was sound. Deep down, she knew that she and Rex weren't a good match. "You're right. He has an irresistible formula. But I know better, and I won't let anything happen."

"Keep telling yourself that, okay?"

"I am. I will."

For however long it took.

At 11:30 p.m., Lisa curled up on the couch with a pillow and blanket, waiting for Rex. He'd called earlier to check on her, but she'd been in class, so he'd talked to her parents. He'd let them know that he'd gotten tied up and would be late. He'd also asked them to stay with her until he got home.

When she heard his car in the driveway, she almost jumped up and ran outside to greet him. But then she controlled her emotions and stayed put.

Waiting…waiting…

He unlocked the front door and came inside. He looked frazzled, and her heart sank. Was something amiss in the case?

He moved forward. "Lisa?" He glanced around. "Where are your parents?"

"They got tired, so I gave them my room. It's the only bed that's big enough for two."

"You should be asleep, too."

"I wanted to wait up for you. I wanted to know how it went."

"It went fine."

"You don't look like it went fine. Did their alibis check out?"

"Actually, they did. Everything they said was true. Nelson was on a plane when the doll incident occurred, and Cathy was at the mall."

"How can you be sure she was there?"

"Some salespeople remember seeing her. Mainly because of Barker. The puppy caused a cute stir wherever he went." Rex stood near the sofa. "Cathy went in and out of stores, then had lunch at La Salsa. She was in the food court around one-thirty."

"Are you certain of the time?"

He nodded. "I was able to view a security tape from that hour, and she was in it."

"So we're back to square one." Not to mention the apology Nelson and Cathy had coming. Lisa felt like a traitor.

"Not exactly."

"What do you mean?" she asked. He had that frazzled look again.

He finally sat next to her. When he made a tight face, she knew something was wrong. Or more wrong. Nothing had been quite right since they'd met.

"You got another threat. Or we both did, I suppose. I dropped by my condo tonight to get my mail and catch up on a few things at home, and there was a package on my doorstep."

A shiver raced up her spine. She suspected the package contained something bloody. She couldn't explain why she felt that way. Maybe it was intuition. Or a manifestation of a very real fear.

He expelled a rough breath. "It was a dead rabbit in one of those hooded receiving blankets. The type you wrap newborns in."

"Was it messy?" Gutted, she thought. Bloody.

"Yes, and it was a white rabbit, like in the Alice story."

She didn't want to envision it, but how could she not? The slaughtered bunny was blinking in her mind. She clutched her stomach, protecting what was hers. And his. The baby belonged to Rex, too.

"There's more," he said.

Lisa kept clutching. "Go on."

Rex turned, facing her all the way, putting them knee to knee. Then he glanced at her tummy, aware of how tightly she was holding on. He looked as if he wanted to hold on, too.

"There were kid's toys in the package, too. You know, those plastic made-in-Japan-supposed-to-be-Indian things. A headdress, a bow and arrow play set, a tomahawk. They were—"

"Smeared in blood?" she asked.

He nodded. "It's becoming apparent that this is racially motivated. Detective Bell thinks so, too."

"You called him? Never mind, of course you did." Still cradling her womb, she grasped for a ray of hope. "Maybe this time the police will get a lead."

"Maybe. I already questioned my neighbors when I was there, but no one saw anyone drop off the package."

"So this is why you called my parents and told them you were running late? Why didn't you just tell them what happened?"

"Because I wanted to talk to you first, and you were unavailable. Besides, I didn't want any of you rushing over to my condo and seeing the rabbit. It's bad enough that I'm putting the image in your head by describing it."

"I'm glad I didn't see it."

"Me, too."

A pause stretched between them. A pregnant pause, she thought.

"Maybe you're wrong, Rex. Maybe this isn't about me. Maybe it's about you. Maybe it's someone you know who's doing it."

"I don't think so and neither does Bell. Leaving the rabbit at my place was a message to me, but the e-mail threat indicates that the perpetrator is closely connected to you. And now that we've established a motive, we think it's someone with white supremacist affiliations. We discovered a historic link between *Snow White and the Seven Dwarfs* and *The Birth of a Nation*."

"*The Birth of a Nation?* I don't know what that is."

"It's a silent film made in 1915 that presents a positive portrayal of the Ku Klux Klan. It was the highest grossing film of its era. But in 1937 *Snow White and the Seven Dwarfs* surpassed it."

"So you think that whoever is threatening our baby used Snow White's name to dethrone her and take back the power of the Klan?"

"Yes, but they're also referencing what happened to you at Disneyland. Between *Snow White* and

*Alice in Wonderland,* they're creating metaphors. The white rabbit is a probably symbolic of saying that the child you're carrying isn't pure. It's all tied together."

"And it's someone from my circle? How can that be? I don't know any white supremacists." Confused and frustrated, she rounded on him. "But I'll bet you do. Surely, the Warrior Society has those types of enemies."

"Yes, we do. But—"

"But what?" She spoke beneath her breath, careful not to wake her parents. "You refuse to acknowledge that this could be coming from you?"

"The evidence says otherwise."

"Oh, really? Then consider us and how different we are. Up until this happened, my life was uneventful. But you're part of an activist organization."

"And so is Kyle. He's the founder, and he's married to an Anglo woman with a mixed-blood baby on the way. If white supremacists were out to destroy our offspring, his wife and child would be targets, too."

"Then there has to be another reason." She refused to believe that he was being impartial. "You promised that you would investigate your side as fully as mine."

"And I will, but not at the expense of the evidence. If I head in the wrong direction, do you know how much time will be wasted? I've been an investigator for a long time. I know my job. And Detective Bell knows his. Between the two of us, we'll get it done."

"By trashing everyone I know and leaving your side unscathed?"

"Dammit, woman. This isn't a competition. I'm trying to keep you safe."

"Safe?" Torn between anger and fear, she wanted to push him away or keep him incredibly close. Either way, she was doomed. "By telling me that I have family or friends who are some sort of secret Klansmen?"

"I'm sorry." He tried to comfort her, reaching for her hand and holding it tightly in his. "I know how scared you are."

"Too much is happening too fast. Every time we turn around, there's another threat."

"I can sleep out here with you tonight. I can take the chair. Or we can snuggle in the guest bed if that'll make you feel better. It'll be a tight fit, but we can make it work."

The bed suggestion drew her in, but she willed it away. Sleeping beside Rex was a danger unto itself.

Still, she wanted him to hold her. Still…nothing. She couldn't let it happen.

"We'll stay out here," she said, fighting off her urges.

If he was disappointed, he didn't let it show. "I'll get changed and grab a pillow and blanket."

He left the room, and she fussed with her own pillow and blanket, trying to get more comfortable on the couch.

When Rex returned, he was bare-chested and wearing a pair of sweatpants. He looked rough and gorgeous.

He dropped his bedding on the chair and came over to her.

"What?" she asked.

"Nothing." He leaned over and tugged her blanket tighter around her. "I just want to look at you."

And touch her, apparently. Lisa got tingly all over.

He glanced down, then back up again. "How long before the baby starts doing things to get your attention?"

"Like move around?" If they had a son, would he grow up to look like his father? Would his eyelashes be long and thick? Would his complexion be warmly bronzed? "Not until the fourth month or so. They say that the first time you feel it move, it's like having butterflies. Not the nervous kind. More of a sweet flutter."

He searched her gaze. "When can the dad put his hand there and feel it move?"

"Soon after the mom feels it, I think. I've heard that some people play womb games. They tap on the mom's tummy so the baby can respond and tap back."

"Really?" He seemed perplexed or fascinated or maybe both. "A fetus will respond like that?"

"So they say."

He smiled a little. "The infamous *they* who knows everything?" He stopped smiling. "I'm sorry I haven't caught the perpetrator yet."

"I know." She wasn't sure what to do or how to feel when he got tender. It was almost easier fighting with him. Her heart ached inside her chest. "Let's go to bed."

"You mean, let's go to couch and chair?" He pulled up on ottoman for his feet, turned out the light and settled into his sleeping space.

But neither of them slept. In the still of the night, in the pitch of what seemed like brutal darkness, they didn't need to compare notes.

They were both thinking about their baby— along with a butchered rabbit and blood-soaked toys that had been left on Rex's doorstep.

## Chapter 8

Two days later, Lisa sat beside Rex in his sporty black hybrid. They were headed to her parents' house for the usual family gathering, and she was apprehensive about it.

She glanced at his profile, analyzing what was about to take place. Rex trusted her parents, but he would be looking at everyone else with a critical eye.

The very idea was preposterous. She would know if someone in her family was racist.

Wouldn't she?

Of course she would. They were people she loved, who loved her, who'd helped raise her. Even

Annabelle, her judgmental eighty-seven-year-old "Auntie," would never condone such a thing.

Lisa turned down the radio, where Justin Timberlake was bringing sexy back. At any other time, she would have welcomed the pulsing beat. "Have you run backgrounds on everyone who's going to be there?"

"Yes."

"And did anything surface?"

"No. But you can't see into someone's soul from a background check. I still want to meet them."

With her hands placed primly on her lap, she lifted her eyebrows. "You can see into other people's souls?"

"I try."

She wondered what he saw in hers. Could he tell that she was fighting her feelings for him? Not just their sexual attraction, but the closeness her mother had warned her about? God, she hoped not. She didn't want him to know that her mixed-up heart was getting involved.

"I can't believe my parents are okay with this," she said, purposely interrupting her own thoughts.

"They're not thrilled about it, but they understand that it's part of my job. All I want to do is meet your extended family and see where they're coming from."

Her defensives were still up. "They're coming

from a good place." And by now, they'd been told about the threats.

"Then quit stressing about it. They know I'm going to be interviewing them."

"Interviewing, yes. Accusing, no."

"I'm not going to accuse anyone to his or her face. If I'm suspicious of someone, I'll investigate further."

"You accused Nelson and Cathy to their faces."

"And I admitted my mistake."

"For all the good it did." The other couple wouldn't accept the apology that had been extended.

He turned onto her parents' street. "Nelson and Cathy will get over it. In another week, she'll be asking for her job back."

She rolled her eyes. "Says the all-knowing P.I."

He parked at the curb. "Just wait and see."

They exited his car and took to the walkway. Lisa's parents lived in the same two-story house where she'd grown up. The cheery yellow structure, hummingbird feeders and carefully trimmed hedges breathed familiarity.

Lisa didn't knock. She simply opened the door, and she and Rex went inside. She guided him into the kitchen and adjoining family room, where everyone gathered. The aroma of pot roast filled the air. Snacks and side dishes cluttered the counters.

Dad greeted them first, then Mom. Overall, there were fourteen people in attendance, including Rex, Lisa and her parents. That left ten for him to interview. No, wait, she thought. Two out of the ten were kids, which left eight.

Gosh, this was making her nervous. All eyes were on her and the handsome investigator at her side. The father of her child. Her one-night stand.

Introductions were made, and Rex seemed to make a favorable impression, except on Auntie. She treated him like an outsider, glaring at him from her wheelchair.

No one said anything about the threats, at least not out loud. But Lisa could tell it was on their minds. Later, of course, Rex would start the interview process. At the moment, he and Lisa were merely socializing with her family. For her, nothing could have been more surreal.

While Rex watched a sporting event on TV with the men, Lisa went into the kitchen to help the women with the meal, and Grandma approached her with a much-needed hug.

"How are you feeling?" the older woman asked.

"I'm still sick in the mornings." And even more restless at night. "But it's supposed to get better."

"It will." Grandma added more milk to the mashed potatoes. She was wearing a classic cook's apron from Williams-Sonoma, embroidered with her name. "Annabelle doesn't trust your young man."

"She doesn't trust anyone. And he isn't mine."

"Then whose is he?"

"No one's. Rex belongs to himself."

"Annabelle is worried that you don't know enough about him, but your mom says that he's doing his best to keep you safe. Thank the Lord for that. Grandpa and I have been praying for you."

"Thank you." Lisa needed all the prayers she could get.

"Have you met his family?"

"They're in North Carolina."

"What about his friends?"

"I haven't met any of them, either. But I'm supposed to. His friend Kyle teaches self-defense, and Kyle's wife, Joyce, is a homicide detective."

"Homicide? Oh, my. Annabelle won't like that."

"Then tell her that they're having a baby, too, only theirs is due this month."

"Oh, that's good. She thinks people should be married to have babies."

"There's another couple Rex talks about. They're not married, but I think they're in a committed relationship. Daniel Deer Runner and Allie Whirlwind. Pretty names, huh?"

Grandma blinked. "Whirlwind? Like the female serial killer?"

Lisa started. "What? Who?"

"Yvonne Whirlwind. She was all over the news. But that was a while ago. I think she's on death row now. Goodness, you don't think Rex's friend is related to her, do you?"

"No, of course not," Lisa responded, when in fact she didn't have a clue.

"I won't mention the Whirlwind girl to Annabelle. I'll just tell her about the baby couple."

"Thanks. No need to rile Auntie any more than she already is."

Soon dinner was ready and everyone gathered around the table. Lisa filled her plate, her thoughts spinning.

Was Allie related to a serial killer? And if she was, why hadn't Rex mentioned it? To her, it seemed extremely relevant. It proved that his friends were far more dangerous than he'd let on. Him and that damn Warrior Society. She was beginning to agree with Annabelle. Just how trustworthy was he?

By the time the meal ended and Rex interviewed Lisa's family, her nerves bundled into knots. All she wanted to do was go home and question him about Allie.

Finally the evening came to a close and they

said their goodbyes. Rex hadn't appeared to make enemies with anyone. Annabelle wagged her finger at him, but he only smiled and leaned over to kiss her cheek.

Did he have no shame? Using his charms on a persnickety old woman?

Lisa sat next to him in the car and pulled the seat belt across her body. Was she jumping to conclusions? Was she being unfair? She honestly didn't know. But between her first-trimester hormones and his casual attitude, she was ready to snap.

"I like your family," he said, as he started the engine. "They're good people."

"I told you they were."

"I know, but I had to find out for myself. Annabelle is a character. She insisted that I was a jerk for bedding you the way I did, then she gave me hell for not asking you to marry me. She wants us to be together."

So much for Auntie's distrust. Apparently he'd won her over. "That's crazy."

"Tell me about it. My mom will probably do that, too, once I tell her about the baby."

Lisa didn't want to sit here and discuss a marriage that was never going to happen.

He spoke again. "Annabelle thinks the perpetrator could be Kirk. She thinks he's a phony, always flaunting his brains in front of everyone. I told her I was already investigating him, but that I would delve deeper."

"Annabelle doesn't know diddly about Kirk. She only dislikes him because he was my boyfriend."

"At least she's trying to help." Rex stopped at a red light. "She also suggested that I take a closer look at Maggie and Tim. She never liked them, either. I'm leery, too. The fact that they found you at Disneyland bothers me. I should have checked them out sooner."

Lisa sighed. Tim and Maggie weren't racists. They were dear friends who'd always treated her like their own.

"You know what else bothers me?" he asked, answering his own question. "That they're on a camping trip with supposedly no phone or Internet access. That's a bit too convenient."

"Right. Their phony alibi." She recalled him mentioning it before. "But how is that convenient? They left before the threats started."

"But not before you announced that you were pregnant."

"So that makes them guilty?"

"It's something to consider."

"If you say so."

The light turned green, and he went through it.

"What's wrong, Lisa? What's going on? Why are you pissed at me again?"

Why, indeed. She sharpened her voice. "Is Allie related to Yvonne Whirlwind? My grandmother recognized the name."

"Oh, for cripes sake. Is that what this is about?" He changed lanes, moving past a pokey car. "Allie is Yvonne's daughter. But that's where the family tie ends. Allie helped put her mother behind bars."

"And you didn't think it was worth mentioning? You're digging around, trying to prove that one of my friends or family is responsible for the threats, and you've got friends with serial killers for parents?"

"Allie's mother has nothing to do with what's happening to us."

"Us? *Us?*" She was shouting now. "You don't give me any rights in this. It's all about what you think should be done, who you think should be investigated."

"Calm down. You'll upset the baby."

"The baby is this big." She held up a space between her thumb and forefinger. "And it can't hear what we're saying."

"Maybe it can."

"Its ears are still forming."

"All the more reason you shouldn't shout."

He was right, and she could've kicked him for it.

She lowered her voice, but her biting tone remained. "Just investigate your side, Rex. Put equal time into the people you know."

"Fine. Now drop it and leave me alone."

He wanted to be left alone? Gladly, she thought.

Once they got home, she marched into the house and retreated to her room, never wanting to speak to him again.

Rex stewed for one full day, ignoring Lisa the way she ignored him.

Finally, on the second day, he arranged for the investigation she kept balking about, then went out and bought her an apology gift. He got something for the baby, too. But he couldn't seem to swallow his pride and give them to her.

On the third day, he got up early, ready to make amends, but his timing was off. Lisa was in the bathroom, going through the morning-sickness thing. Feeling badly for her, he went into the kitchen to fix some food. He knew how famished she got after the nausea passed.

Later, when she emerged, he was putting the finishing touches on breakfast, slicing fruit for the oatmeal. The eggs were already done and so was the decaffeinated cappuccino she favored.

"What's going on?" she asked.

"I cooked," he responded.

"For both of us?"

"Of course for both of us. Well, mainly for you. I'm sorry we've been fighting, and I'm sorry I haven't taken your concerns more seriously." He dispensed the coffee and handed her a cup. "I asked another P.I. to investigate my side. I figured it was better to have someone else do it, someone who could be more objective." And it wouldn't cut into Rex's time or take away from what he considered the primary investigation. He hadn't changed his mind about the case, but he owed Lisa the courtesy she'd requested.

"Thank you." She sipped the cappuccino. Post-sick pale, but as pretty as ever, she was dressed in girlie pink pajamas. "I'm sorry we've been fighting, too. I'm not usually this emotional."

"You're pregnant, and someone is threatening you and the baby." Making Rex want to annihilate the son of a bitch. "Who wouldn't be emotional?"

"I've been sleeping even worse since we've been fighting."

"Me, too." He hadn't been able to get her off his mind. He gestured to the dining-room table. "Are you ready to eat?"

"Yes, please."

She gathered the flatware, and he carried their

plates. After breakfast, he would shed even more of his pride and give her the gifts he'd brought.

He sat across from her. He knew that her parents would be going to the studio with her today. He'd meant what he'd said about everyone in her family. They were good people, and they loved her dearly.

His family loved him, too, but it seemed different. Her family was well-adjusted and happy. They didn't bicker among themselves.

She dived into her breakfast. "You're a pretty good cook."

"Who can't scramble eggs? Or follow the directions on an oatmeal box? Or pop bread in the toaster?"

"You put cheese, tomatoes and onions in the eggs. That takes creativity. The fruit for the oatmeal was a nice touch, too."

"You do all of that kind of stuff. I was only mimicking you."

She smiled. "Then you're a good mimic."

"I like having home-cooked meals with you." He was getting used to the coziness that seemed to go with it. "When I'm alone, I eat out most of the time. I guess it's the bachelor in me."

Speaking of going out...

He shifted in his chair. "I still owe you a date."

She lifted her coffee, and the cup hid part of her face. "I'm ready anytime you are."

"We could go to the Southwest Museum. They're having a jewelry show this weekend."

"That would be fun. Is that an American Indian museum?"

He nodded. "It'll be a great place to take our kid when he or she is older. They have lots of activities for children."

"That sounds nice, Rex. Really nice."

It wasn't the Cherokee Fair, he thought. But it would do. "We can make a day of it. We can come back and change afterward, then go to a dinner club. Someplace classy where we can dance. Does that sound all right?"

"Totally." She all but beamed.

After breakfast, he said, "I have something for you. And for the baby. Wait here and I'll get it."

"Okay." She seemed pleasantly surprised.

He darted into the guest room and retrieved the items, both of which were wrapped in fancy gift bags and topped with audacious bows.

When he returned, Lisa was standing in the exact same spot. She'd taken him literally about where to wait.

"This is yours." He handed her the glittery gold bag. "And this is for the kid." He turned over the one with teddy bears on it. "But I guess it's obvious which is which."

She clutched both of them against her chest. "What made you do this?"

"I felt badly about our fight." And he felt awkward now. "Just so you know, the gift-wrapping department at the store came up with those bags."

"They're pretty. Does it matter which one I open first?"

"Not really. Well, maybe a little. Open yours first."

She placed the baby's gift on the counter and peeked into hers, opening it carefully. Good thing, he thought. The item inside of it was glass.

She unwrapped the tissue and lifted the figurine. He'd chosen a handsome male fairy with long black hair and rugged wings.

"Oh, Rex. He's beautiful."

"He's not from the Cherokee Little People, but I thought he looked sort of how they would look, except for the wings."

She admired her gift. "My girl fairies are going to love him."

He smiled, then laughed. "Love him how? Like they're gonna have this big, sparkly orgy?"

*"Rex."* She reprimanded him, but she laughed, too. Then she said a very sincere "Thank you."

"You're welcome. Now open the other one."

She set down the fairy, handling him like a special little being. To her, he was real. But Rex understood. He'd been raised on magic, make-believe and otherwise.

Lisa opened the baby's gift, removing a stuffed toy in the shape of a butterfly.

Her eyes turned misty. "You bought this because of what I said, didn't you? That the first little movement will feel like butterfly wings."

He nodded, and she hugged him.

Her hair tickled his cheek, and her body fit snugly against his. He wished he had the courage to lift her pajama top and put his hand on her stomach. But he was still fighting that kind of connection, afraid of the bond it would create. Besides, what would he feel, aside from her bare skin?

For now, that was better left undone.

# Chapter 9

The Southwest Museum was a wondrous place. Lisa walked beside Rex, going in and out of rooms and soaking up the displays. She discovered that the museum had undergone extensive changes in the past few years, including the conservation of its collections, some of which had been damaged from water leaking into the original building. There had also been structural damage from an earthquake. Overall, the museum had been in desperate need of the grants it had received.

It was beautiful now. The building had been renovated, with five times the previous gallery space.

When Lisa and Rex came to the area showcasing the Eastern Woodland Indians, she touched her tummy. The Cherokee were one of the most well-known of the Woodland tribes, and the artifacts on display were part of her child's ancestry.

Standing beside Rex, she looked through a glass enclosure with decoy masks. Some had been constructed to stalk wild game and some had been used in what was called the Booger Dance, where men from the tribe dressed up and performed comical gyrations.

The next enclosure held pots and bowls. The double-sided wedding vase caught her eye. In earlier times, Rex probably would have been obligated to marry her.

"They used to break those to seal their vows," he said, acting as her tour guide. "Some traditionalists still practice those old ceremonies."

"It's fascinating." Confused by the effect the vase was having on her, she blew out the breath she was holding. She hoped that she wasn't falling in love. For her, that would spell disaster. Rex Sixkiller wasn't the marrying kind. He'd admitted it more than once.

The next enclosure offered wedding attire, which was both beautiful and primitive.

He approached the case. "They used to exchange food instead of rings."

"You know a lot about ancient Cherokee weddings."

"It varied from clan to clan, but I know the basics. I know a bit about ancient Cherokee childbirth, too."

She moved closer. "Like what?"

"The mother knelt on a robe to give birth, and afterward, the father or nearest relative buried the placenta. Also, the Cherokee weren't known to use cradleboards." He indicated a painting on the wall, depicting a woman with a baby tied inside of a blanket on her back. "That's how they did it."

"You can buy stuff like that now. Slings, pouches and tie carriers. For the front and the back."

He smiled. "That'd be cool."

"It would, wouldn't it?" The idea appealed to her. But suddenly it made her afraid, too. Not of carrying the baby, but of what would happen if the perpetrator succeeded in destroying the life in her womb and she never got the chance to hold it.

Rex noticed her expression. "Don't do that, Lisa."

"Do what?"

"Think about the threats." He slipped his arms around her. "Our child is going to be fine. He's going to grow up strong and healthy."

She practically fell into his embrace. It felt incredibly good to be held by him. "He?"

"Or she. It was a figure of speech."

He put his forehead against hers. She wanted him to kiss her, but she knew that he wouldn't. When he'd asked her out, he'd sworn to behave on their date. Regardless, he was creating warmth and intimacy, and it made her crave more of him.

Was she falling in love? Lisa didn't have anything to compare it to. She hadn't been in love with Jamie or Kirk, not in the true sense of the emotion. Already the depth of what she felt for Rex exceeded what she'd felt for those other men.

He stepped back, but he continued to watch her, to analyze her. She returned his searching gaze, her heartbeat accelerating.

"I'm okay now," she said. She wasn't, not completely, but she was going to try to improve her state of mind. As for her heart, she had no idea how to make it stop beating so fast.

"Are you sure?"

"Yes." What else could she do but reassure him? "Sometimes it's tough not to think about the case."

"I wasn't going to discuss it with you today, but maybe I should."

"Why? Is something going on?"

"Yes, with Kirk. I came across an article he wrote for the company he works for. It appeared in an old newsletter. It was about the history of African

Americans on Wall Street. It was sensitively written and not something that someone with racist affiliations would address, at least not in the way he addressed it."

"I knew he wasn't the perpetrator."

"I'm inclined to agree."

"So who are you targeting now? Tim and Maggie? It isn't going to be them, either."

"We'll see. And just so you know, nothing damaging has surfaced from my side, and I told my colleague to dig deep."

"It's only been a few days," she said, then added, "I'm sorry. I didn't mean that the way it sounded."

"I understand. Neither of us wants to admit that it's someone we're close to. But it is."

"You don't believe it's someone you're close to, Rex. You're certain it's coming from my side." And somewhere in the pit of her soul, she feared that he was right. But she couldn't accept it. Not until she knew for certain.

"There's something else I should probably mention."

Her nerves kicked up a notch. "What?"

"Everyone at your studio is white. The employees, the students. I noticed it, and so did the police."

"That isn't intentional. My studio is located in a white neighborhood." Not far from the neighborhood where she lived, which she realized was white, too. "It's the area where I grew up."

"I'm not accusing you of anything. But here's the thing, the perpetrator and/or perpetrators probably thought it was intentional. They probably thought you shared their views until you slept with me and decided to keep the baby."

More proof that it was coming from her side?

She said, "I can't imagine anyone I know being a white supremacist."

"You could've missed the signs, especially if you weren't looking for them. But why don't we drop it for now?" He gestured toward the exit. "Do you want to go outside and check the jewelry show? That's what we came here for."

"Yes. Absolutely." She could certainly use a breath of fresh air.

Side by side, they wandered among tables that had been set up on the lawn. Just a short distance away, a Native man in colorful regalia was telling stories to a circle of children. Parents listened, too.

The atmosphere was festive, and every so often Rex would reach for her hand.

"Let me buy you something," he said.

She thought about the fairy. "You just got me a gift."

"That doesn't mean I can't get you something

else. Look at all this stuff. There are some great items to choose from."

He was right. The tables were filled with silver jewelry, decorated with turquoise and other ornamental stones. The pieces that drew her attention were made by the Zuni, a tribe that was known for its elaborate designs and carved fetishes.

"I like this style the best." She gestured to a tray of necklaces that were colorful, as well as intricate, with tiny stones creating beautiful patterns.

"You've got good taste," Rex said. "That's called petit point."

Like the stitch in needlepoint, she thought.

The white trader representing the jewelry smiled, and Lisa checked the prices and realized that she was browsing his most expensive collection.

She tried to backpedal, rather than spend too much of Rex's money, but he steered her toward a delicate red coral pendant with a hefty price tag.

When she turned it over, she noticed the artist's stamp on the back. The trader told her that the artist was a young man from the Zuni reservation, with a wife and a new baby. That seemed to please Rex.

He bought the pendant, then stood quietly behind her, latching it around her neck.

"This is good karma," he said, sounding more like a Buddhist than a Cherokee.

She closed her eyes. His breaths were tickling her skin. "Because we're helping a young family with a baby?"

"Yes." He released the chain on the pendant.

When she turned around to face him, her emotions intensified. By the time they left the museum and headed home to change for dinner, Lisa was steeped in everything Rex.

The color of his eyes. The thickness of his hair. The scent of his cologne.

He seemed steeped in her, too.

"You look gorgeous," he said, when she emerged, ready for the second phase of their date.

"Thank you." She was wearing a skirt and blouse ensemble, cinched with a belt and accented with red pumps. She'd chosen an outfit that complemented her new necklace. She wanted the good karma to continue.

He roamed his gaze over her. "Great legs. Killer shoes."

Her skirt was short and her heels were high. "I'm a sexy mom tonight."

"I'll say." He looked as if he wanted to ravage her where she stood.

But he didn't, of course. Instead, they both turned momentarily quiet. To combat the erotic tension, she said, "I won't be able to wear the skirt and shoes for too much longer, but the blouse will still work."

He tilted his head, looking at her from a different angle. "You're going to turn it into a makeshift maternity top?"

Self-conscious, she fussed with the tails. "It's puffy without the belt."

"Damn. It's actually starting to seem hot."

"What is?"

"You getting a baby bump." He did the eye roaming thing again, checking her out from top to bottom, then settling on the still-flat area in the middle.

Lisa's pulse blasted through her pregnant body. "You're just trying to be nice."

"I bought you presents to be nice. This is—"

"Weird?" she provided, trying to lighten the conversation.

"Totally weird. Baby bumps aren't supposed to be sexy."

"Says who?"

"Guys like me."

He moved closer, and the air between them sizzled. She wanted to grab hold of him, press her body against his and kiss him with all of her pre-baby-bump might.

"I want to touch it," he said quietly. "I want to put my hand there."

Lisa knew he meant her stomach. Her bare stomach. In response, she removed her belt and let it slide to the floor.

She considered lifting her blouse for him, but she stood idle, waiting for him to make the next move.

He did, a bit cautiously. He reached out and gathered the tails of her shirt, raising the garment one thread at a time.

"I've thought about this so many times," he said. "But I kept holding back."

"Because getting that close to the baby scared you?"

He nodded. "It still does."

But regardless, he slipped his hand under the material, which was now bunched at her waist. The connection was soft and gentle, but erotic, too. His thumb skimmed her belly button.

"Hey, little one," he said. "This is your daddy."

Lisa watched him, captivated by his introduction. He was a fascinating man, a newfound father, and she wanted him so badly, she ached in unmentionable places.

Rex looked up, and their gazes locked. She decided to take a chance, to take what she so desperately wanted. With a deep breath, she leaned forward, initiating a kiss.

As her lips found his, he reacted in kind, opening his mouth against hers.

Lisa accepted the invitation and kissed him the way only a woman on the brink of insanity could.

While their tongues collided, he fanned his fingers across her stomach. She imagined that he was painting a rainbow across their baby's heart.

He tasted hot and spicy, and all she wanted was more.

More…

More…

When they came up for air, he said, "We're not supposed to be doing this."

"I know. It's crazy." Sexy crazy. Beautiful crazy. "But I don't want to stop."

"Me, neither."

Their mouths came together again, and she lost herself in the moment. While he touched her stomach, she maneuvered her way around him and unbuttoned her blouse.

That caught his attention, and he ended the kiss. He stepped back to study her. By now, her top was completely open, her black lacy bra exposed, her navel bare.

"Are you sure you want to go that far?" he asked.

"Yes." There was no turning back. She wanted to be with him.

His voice all but vibrated. "I promised that I would be a gentleman. That I wouldn't take advantage—"

"You're not taking anything. I'm giving it to you."

"You won't get shy in the morning? You won't regret it?"

"No." There was no room for shyness, for regret. No room for falling in love, either. She would fight those feelings, jagged tooth and ragged nail. "I just want you inside me."

He unbuttoned his shirt, baring a portion of his flesh and putting them on equal ground. "I'm going to owe you another night on the town."

"Another date?" She glanced at his flat brown nipples, then lowered her gaze, following the masculine trail that led to the waistband of his pants. "I almost forgot that we were on our way out."

"Now we're on our way to bed." He drew her into his arms and kissed her again.

She gripped his shoulders, seduced by the breadth of them. Rex Sixkiller was all passion, all tall, dark and Y chromosome.

They stumbled to her room, kissing the entire way. Inside the dimly lit chamber, the fairy figurines glittered, and she could've sworn the girls were dancing around the lone male. The orgy Rex had teased her about.

And why not, she thought, as he lowered her onto the bed and she kicked off her shoes. Magic was in the air.

He stripped her, removing every stitch of clothing. He took special care with her bra and panties, and when she was naked, he flicked his tongue over one nipple, then the other, taunting her with his desire.

Soon he was moving his way down her body. He stopped to plant a devoted-daddy kiss on her tummy, and she marveled at his sweetness, until he tongued her navel and made her moan.

He was still fully clothed. Aside from his unbuttoned shirt, he hadn't undressed.

As he parted her legs and put his mouth against her, she arched her back, dizzily aroused. He hadn't done this to her during their one-night stand, and he was making up for lost time.

He teased her most sensitive spot, making naughty, nibbling forays. Pressure built in her loins and fire scorched the blood running thickly through her veins.

A climax was brewing.

She looked down and watched him. He was intent on making her come. As the spasms started, she tugged at his hair, thinking how wicked he was.

Lost in the feeling, she closed her eyes and let it happen.

Only there was no quiet afterglow.

When the wave subsided and she could breathe, he pushed her to the brink again, giving her a repeat performance.

"One, two," she whispered, preparing for a second orgasm.

*"Saquu, tali."*

He counted off in what she assumed were the same numbers in his ancestors' language. What a time for a Cherokee lesson.

"You're torturing me," she panted.

"That's the idea," he responded, making her warmer and wetter.

And desperate for him to get naked, too.

## Chapter 10

Rex sat up and looked at Lisa. He had no idea how a woman could be so wholesome yet so incredibly sensual. She was like one of her fairies come to life, only with endless legs instead of sparkly wings.

As she reached for him, his erection strained against his zipper. They rolled over the bed and kissed, peeling off his clothes and discarding them in disarray.

She roamed his shoulders, his chest, his stomach, as if she wasn't sure what part of him to touch first. He didn't care where she put her hands, as long as they were on his aroused body.

She pressed her cheek against his abs. "I want to—"

His breath hitched. "What?"

"Do what you did to me." She lowered her head and tasted the tip of him with her tongue.

Heaven on earth.

Should he stop her?

Without giving himself a rational moment to answer, he tangled his hands in her hair, wrapping his fingers around the silky strands.

As always, she was ladylike, even in the midst of something so primal. He watched her make him bigger and harder.

Sensation slammed into sensation. She was milking him for all he was worth, and he was worth plenty.

Plenty of heat...

Plenty of spark...

She ignited him from the inside out, from the outside in. Maybe he should stop her. Maybe he—

She went deeper.

"Lisa," he ground out.

"Rex." She paused and said his name, too. Only she added the rest of it, and hearing her say "Six-killer" while he was cocked and loaded made him feel like a gunslinger.

She kept pleasuring him, over and over, using her hands and her mouth. Finally, before he lost complete control, he lifted her up.

By now, even his brain was on fire.

Encouraging her to straddle him, he guided her onto his lap. This was one of the positions they'd mastered on their first night together, and he was desperate for an encore.

But before she sank onto him, he asked, "Do we need a condom?" He gave her the option of putting a barrier between them, even if she was already pregnant.

She refused the protection. "I want to feel you. Only you."

Flesh-to-flesh, she was impaled by him. She tipped her head back, and he fought for survival, especially when she sucked her bottom lip between her teeth. It made her look naughty yet innocent.

Wholesome. Sensual.

Up and down she went, and as her breasts rose and fell, he circled her waist. Together they created a hot, wet ride.

Damn, but he loved sex. She seemed to love it, too. Or maybe she just loved it with him. He hoped so. He liked being the object of her lust.

Kissing her hard and fast, he nudged her down, switching to a missionary position. He slid between her thighs, and she wrapped her dancer's legs around him.

Good and tight.

He never wanted the feeling to end. They forged an emotional joining; they made wild love.

He looked into her eyes. "Are we going to keep doing this later? Are we going to keep being lovers?"

"You mean, after you're not living here anymore?"

"Yes."

She made a soft, breathy sound. "If you want to."

"I do." He filled himself with her fragrance, inhaling her misty perfume. "Do you?"

She nodded, her nails digging into his skin. While she clawed his back, he increased the bed-hammering rhythm.

She came right before he went off, right before he thrust one last soul-rocketing time and spilled into her.

Sexual synchronicity.

Spent, he waited a beat and collapsed in her arms. She held him, accepting the full weight of his body.

He inhaled her skin, as he'd done before, only now it was a combination of her pretty perfume and his post-sex pheromones.

Lethal to the last scent.

Finally he rolled onto his side. Slick with sweat, they faced each other.

Had he just made a commitment, admitting that he wanted to remain lovers?

Yes, no, maybe? He wasn't sure. But what difference would it make if they kept sleeping together? They were already bonded. She was carrying his child.

"One day at a time," he said, making his intentions known. It wasn't as if he was going to marry her.

She leaned on her elbow, and the pale bedroom light cast angelic shadows across her body, softening her nakedness. "Are you talking about our relationship?"

He nodded, being as honest as he could. "No serious strings attached. Except for the baby."

"That works for me. Lord knows, I don't want to fall for you."

She'd already given this some thought? Curious as he was, he wasn't about to ask how deeply she'd considered it. As long as they were on the same page, it was better not to know. He reached out and put his hand on her stomach, touching the tie that bound them.

*"Kamama,"* he said.

"What does that mean?"

"Butterfly. But in some contexts it means elephant."

"That's great." She scrunched up her face. "It's a butterfly now and an elephant when I get bigger?"

He kept his hand softly in place. He wasn't making fun of her. "Elephants have butterfly-shaped ears."

"That sounds better."

"*Kamama* is a name, too, but only for the prettiest of girls." He gazed at the woman with whom he'd just been intimate. "Of course if we have a girl, she'll be as pretty as you are."

"Thank you." Her smile was sweet. "What if we have a boy? What would you call him?"

"How about *Atsutsa?*"

"What does that mean?"

He grinned. "Boy."

"Oh, that's clever." She play punched his ribs, and they both laughed.

Afterward, Rex gave her a tender kiss. She was still bathed in an ethereal light: golden hair, fair skin, pink nipples.

He imagined their baby at her breast, then ran his hands down the sides of her body, molding her curves and making her quaver.

"Make love with me again," he said, needing her.

She moved closer, apparently needing him, too. He climbed on top of her and cuffed her wrists with his hands. When he let go, their fingers linked.

And stayed that way.

All through the night.

Lisa had been Rex's lover for two days, and she was doing fine. Or as fine as a pregnant woman fighting her feelings could be.

But this evening her semblance of fineness vanished. While she was at the studio, with her parents acting as her bodyguards or babysitters or whatever, Rex had called. He'd told her to bring her parents home with her, instead of them dropping her off like they normally did.

Rex would be waiting to speak to all of them.

"It must be bad," Dad said, as he pulled into Lisa's driveway. "Or he wouldn't have been so cryptic."

Had there been another threat? More violent than the last? Lisa glanced at her mom, who'd volunteered to sit in the backseat. She seemed to be thinking the same thing.

Dad put the car in Park and killed the engine. They exited the vehicle and went into the house.

Rex popped up from the couch and approached them. He looked at Lisa, and they exchanged a couple's gaze. She could tell that he wanted to hold her, to comfort her, to make her less afraid of whatever he was about to reveal, but he kept a proper distance in front of her parents. Lisa hadn't told them that she was sleeping with him.

It didn't matter. Mom noticed. But for now, there were bigger issues at hand.

"Why don't we sit on the porch," Rex said.

Lisa agreed with his suggestion. The walls of her little house seemed to be closing in.

"I'd like to make some tea first." Mom insisted on brewing an herbal drink.

Lisa agreed with that suggestion, too. Tea and honey might help calm her nerves.

While Mom went into the kitchen, Lisa and the men waited on the porch. A light breeze blew, making leaves on the lone tree in the yard stir.

"It's a nice night," Dad said, filling the silence.

Rex nodded, and Lisa wanted to reach for his hand. But she didn't. She just sat at the table, gazing at the tree.

Mom finally appeared with a serving tray. She'd prepared tea for everyone.

Lisa sweetened hers and took a sip. So did Mom. The men didn't drink theirs. No one had asked them if they'd wanted it, but it was the thought that counted.

"This is about Maggie and Tim," Rex said. "I discovered that they belong to a church associated with white supremacy. They've been part of the same group for over thirty years. The name of the church has changed since then, and the leader claims it no longer has those ties. But I think that's a front to protect its members."

"Does it have a history of violence?" Dad asked.

"Yes, though nothing lately. But that doesn't mean that hatred isn't being taught behind closed doors. Most of these types of churches claim to pursue legal, nonviolent means to attain their goals, so it wouldn't matter if they admitted who and what they are. Freedom of religion is protected by the First Amendment."

"I've met some of their church friends," Mom said, clearly struggling to take it all in. "And they seemed like average people."

"As opposed to what?" Rex asked. "The skinheads and white-robe-wearing types you've seen on TV? It isn't always like that."

"Obviously." Dad's shoulders tensed. "So are Maggie and Tim the bastards trying to hurt our girl?"

Rex responded, "It certainly seems so, but I don't have any proof."

Mom gave a shudder. "They've been sending cruel e-mails and leaving vile things in cars and on doorstops? I thought they loved us. I thought they loved our daughter." Her voice vibrated. "How naive could we be, not knowing how evil they were? How evil they are."

Lisa thought about her white neighborhood, her white studio, her mostly white world. "We lived in a bubble."

Mom cleared her throat. "We don't anymore."

Rex went quiet, and Lisa glanced at her lover. A stream of emotion stretched between them, and suddenly she could tell that he had more on his mind, that what he'd shared was only the tip of the iceberg.

She clutched her tea and the cup felt breakable in her hand. But everything seemed breakable now. "What else is going on?"

He frowned. "I don't know how to say it."

"Not saying it is worse." She couldn't imagine what it was, and now the anticipation was tightening her stomach. She hoped the baby couldn't feel the pressure.

"I'm going to try to collect some DNA on Maggie and Tim. But I'll need to go to their house to get it." He turned to her mom. "I'd like to use the key they left with you."

The older woman nodded, and Lisa relaxed. Going to Maggie and Tim's house wasn't something to panic about. Mom had been watering their plants and collecting their mail. It wouldn't cause suspicion.

"How will their DNA help?" Dad asked. "I thought they didn't leave anything behind at the crime scenes."

"They didn't."

After Rex responded to her dad, he shifted his gaze to Lisa, and the panic returned. He was looking at her in a way that spoke of trouble, of pain, of everything in between.

What? she thought. *What?*

He finally said in a clear strong voice, "It's possible that Maggie and Tim are your biological parents. That they—"

"No!" She cut him off, refusing to hear the rest of what he had to say. By now, her heart was pounding a horribly brutal rhythm. "That makes no sense."

"I'm sorry. I understand how disturbing this is, but it isn't something I came up with on a whim. I discussed it at length with the police, and they agree that it's a possibility."

Dad crossed his arms in front of his chest in that "Stone Cold" wrestler way of his, and Mom looked ready to cry. Lisa fought tears, too. She wanted to tell Rex to go away and never come back. But of course, she didn't.

Don't shoot the messenger, she thought, especially if you're already half in love with him.

Rex tried to explain. "Given the circumstances, it seems doubtful that Tim and Maggie being at Disneyland that day was a coincidence. I think they'd been following your family, going wherever you went. And there has to be a reason for that."

"If I'm their child, then why didn't they keep me?" Lisa argued. "Why chase me around instead?"

"Maybe they changed their minds about the adoption, but it was too late to get you back. Or maybe they lost custody of you and one of their relatives gave you up. Or maybe the state was involved."

"So once I was gone, they tracked me down, followed my new family and used the incident at Disneyland as a way to insinuate themselves into our lives?" She refused to give credence to his theory. "That's ludicrous."

"Is it?" he challenged.

Lisa's mind whirred. Did she look like Tim and Maggie? No, she thought. Except for that Tim was tall and trim and Maggie was blone. She glanced at her parents for reassurance, but they were gazing at each other. Were they trying to decide if it could be true?

Rex said, "If Maggie and Tim gave you up, then found a way to be part of your life, it provides an even deeper motive for the threats."

She didn't respond. What if they really were her biological family? She didn't want their blood flowing through her veins.

Mom reached for Dad's hand, and they both turned toward the P.I. They didn't say anything, but they seemed to respect his judgment. They weren't fighting him.

Lisa was. She held fast to her stubbornness, her fear. "They might be the perpetrators, but they aren't my biological parents." She wouldn't let them be, even if they'd always treated her as if she had belonged to them.

The timbre of Rex's voice was soft, but his words seemed harsh. "If that isn't who they are, then who are they really? Why were they at Disneyland when you were a little girl? And why did they befriend your family?"

"They were sick strangers who got unnaturally attached to me."

"Yes, they're sick, but I don't believe they were strangers and neither do the police. But there's no way to be sure without unlocking the past. Until I know who they are and what's truly going on inside their heads, it's going to be tough to prove my case. They're not going to stay on a phony vacation forever, and when they come back, I want to be armed with something to use against them."

"They're supposed to return the Saturday after next," Mom said.

Rex nodded. Apparently he was already aware of Tim and Maggie's supposed schedule.

Unnerved, Lisa looked away. He didn't understand how this was making her feel. He claimed to know how disturbing it was, but how could he? His identity wasn't on the line.

Mom opened her purse and gave Rex the key, and Lisa continued to stare into space. This wasn't the legacy she wanted to leave to her child.

What would happen if she refused to give Rex

her DNA? Would he take it from somewhere in her house, too?

"I'm sorry," he said, causing her to look at him. "But I'm doing this to help keep you safe."

"We all are," Mom added.

"It has to be done," Dad interjected.

"I know." Yet knowing didn't make her any less afraid of what might turn out to be a very ugly truth. But at least it couldn't get any worse.

Could it?

When a chill passed through her bones, she wrapped her arms around herself, fighting whatever storm lay ahead.

# *Chapter 11*

Lisa insisted on going with Rex to collect the potential DNA samples. She wanted to walk through Tim and Maggie's house and dismiss her old memories of them. She wanted to look around and see them for the heartless people they were.

As they approached the front door, she asked, "What if they come home and catch us?"

"They're not going to take the chance of coming home and letting their neighbors see them. They're still supposed to be on vacation."

Lisa looked around. There wasn't a neighbor in sight. "But what if they show up anyway?"

"Then I'll shoot them."

At any other time she might've laughed, but there was nothing funny about the situation she was in. She glanced at the gun clipped to his belt. "Better them than us."

"Damn straight." He unlocked the door, and they crossed the threshold.

Lisa had been inside Tim and Maggie's house many times before, but now it seemed haunted. The decor was direct, with dark blue sofas and oak tables. Greenery was abundant. On a wrought iron plant rack, potted vines twined around the shelves.

Maggie worked at a nursery, Tim was an electrician. Normal people on the outside, Lisa thought, and monsters within.

Rex put on a pair of latex gloves. "Is the kitchen this way?"

She nodded, and they headed in that direction.

"Damn," he said, when he saw the empty sink. He opened the dishwasher, and it was empty, too. No dirty glasses or unwashed eating utensils.

Lisa noticed the herbs on the windowsill. They were flourishing. "Maggie taught me to garden, and Tim used to give me piggyback rides. Now everything they did seems like a lie. If they're my biological parents, then this is their grandchild." She touched her tummy. "How could they threaten to kill their own grandbaby? How could they mangle a doll? Or gut a poor little rabbit? How could they be that cruel?"

Rex moved to stand beside her. "I shouldn't have let you come here."

"No, it's okay. I needed to."

"But look how it's affecting you."

"I knew it would."

"Then let's get what we came for and get out of here."

Together, they entered the master bedroom and the connecting bathroom, where more plants flourished.

In the backyard, she knew, was a vegetable garden. Now Lisa wanted to go home and dig up her garden. Or better yet, go outside and destroy all of Maggie's hard work. But what would that accomplish? Rage would get her nowhere.

"Bingo," Rex said.

He collected two drinking glasses on the counter. There were no combs or brushes. Maggie and Tim must have packed them. He kept looking and plucked strands of blond hair from a curling iron that had been left behind.

"Do you think they're staying at a motel?" Lisa asked.

"No. They're probably camping, just as they said they would be, using the supplies they packed and keeping a low profile. But they're somewhere local. That way, they can come into town to do their dirty deeds and take off again."

"What about the e-mail?"

"Bell is checking to see if anyone from their congregation is a tech or possibly a hacker, someone who could've helped them. Whoever routed that e-mail was a pro."

This wasn't good news. "Then someone else is involved in threatening me?"

"Not necessarily. Whoever helped them might have done it as favor to Maggie and Tim, rather than an act of aggression toward you. They might not even be aware that it was intended as a threat. Of course that doesn't mean that they won't cover for Maggie and Tim, especially if it's someone from their church."

She watched him rummage through the cabinets. "How long are the DNA tests going to take?"

"A day or so."

"Really? That soon?"

"Normally the results take five to ten days, but I can have the lab put a rush on it. The director is a colleague of mine."

"Who isn't?" she teased.

He shrugged, smiled. "It comes with the territory." He met her gaze, and they turned silent for a moment. Then he said, "I'll swab the inside of your cheek when we get home."

To collect her DNA, she thought. "Does Detective Bell know that you're doing this?"

Rex nodded and continued to look for more samples. Apparently he wasn't taking any chances. He seemed determined to provide the lab with as many items as possible, to make sure that what was extracted from them was viable.

They went into the other bathroom, but it was clear that no one used it except for guests.

"Does Tim or Maggie smoke?" he asked.

"He does. But not in the house. He smokes on the patio."

They headed outside, and Rex found cigarette butts in an ashtray and bagged them.

Lisa gazed out at the garden she wanted to destroy. At this time of year, tomatoes and peppers were the primary plants. "Why do you think they're willing to take such a risk? Aren't they worried that you or the police will figure it out? Look how easily you uncovered information about their church."

"We're figuring it out, but all we have so far is circumstantial evidence."

"And that's what Tim and Maggie are counting on?" A lump formed in her throat. "Proof that guilty people can go free?"

He turned to face her and removed his gloves. "They're not going to go free."

She didn't respond. She knew he had every intention of keeping the promises he'd been making to her, but what if Tim and Maggie succeeded anyway? What if Lisa lost the baby she was carrying? The stress alone could cause her to miscarry.

*Brrring!*

Rex's cell phone rang and he checked the display screen to see who it was.

He answered it, and Lisa listened to the one-sided conversation.

"Hey," he said. "What's up?"

Pause. Talking on the other end.

An upbeat tone. "Oh, man. That's great. You must be over the moon."

More talking on the other line.

An unsure tone. "Tomorrow? I don't know. We'll try." A glance at Lisa. "I'll have to see how my lady is doing."

His lady? Whatever it was involved her?

"Okay," he said, ending the call. "Congratulations, brother. Save me a cigar."

Suddenly the conversation became clear. "Was that Kyle? Did his wife have their baby? How much did she weigh? What did they name her?"

He answered one question at a time. "Yes, it was

Kyle. And yes, Joyce had their baby. She's six pounds, eight ounces, healthy as a little horse and her name is Patricia Ann Prescott."

"Oh, that's sweet." She angled her head, wondering about what he'd told Kyle. "What did you mean you'd have to see how your lady is doing?"

"He wants us to come by the birthing center tomorrow. Allie and Daniel are going over about eleven, and he thought it'd be nice for all of us to be there at the same time. But I wasn't sure if you would be up for it."

"Of course I am." She wanted to congratulate the first-time parents, but more importantly she wanted to see the baby, to take joy in a new life. And try to forget, if only for a moment, that the child she'd conceived with Rex was in danger.

"You're not going to be uncomfortable around Allie because of who her mother is?"

"I probably would have been before. But now? Who am I to judge her? Look who my parents might be."

"I'm sorry, Lisa. I wish I could make it better."

"You can. Going to see Joyce and Kyle's baby will make it better."

"Okay, but we'll have to stop by the lab first and drop off the samples."

"Do your friends know about everything that's

going on with us? That I'm pregnant and being threatened?"

"Yes, they know." He placed his hand on her stomach, tender as could be, comforting her and the baby.

Lisa looped her arms around his neck, and soon they were kissing full-force on the mouth, taking refuge in each other.

"I like that you called me your lady," she said.

"I like that you're her."

Was this how most one-day-at-a-time relationships played out? She had no idea. But later that night when he led her to bed, she went willingly.

And warned herself, as always, not to fall completely in love.


The birthing center was beautiful. As soon as Lisa and Rex entered the lobby of the building, she felt a sense of home and hearth.

"This is a nice facility," Rex said. He was carrying flowers for Joyce and a feather inside of a small cedar box for Kyle. "Maybe we should consider having our little one here."

"Maybe we should." It was certainly more inviting than a clinical hospital setting. "I'll talk to my doctor about it."

After they checked in with the reception desk and

headed in the direction of Joyce and Kyle's room, she asked, "Are you going to be there when our baby is born?"

"Of course I am."

"So you're going to be my birthing coach?"

He stopped walking and turned to look at her. "I hadn't thought about that."

She quickly dismissed him. She wasn't going to force him into taking on a role that would make him uneasy. "That's okay, my mom can do it."

"No. I want to. There's just been so much else going on, I hadn't considered that part. Won't I have to take classes or something?"

Grateful for his interest, she smiled. She adored her mom, but having Rex attend the birth would make her feel like less of a single parent and more like a family. "Yes, but not until the time gets closer."

"I should go with you when they do the ultrasound, too. Kyle carried around the ultrasound picture of his kid in his wallet. She looked like an alien." He pondered the thought. "What if she still looks like one?"

Lisa laughed. "She won't."

"Yeah, but what if she does? We're going to have to say she's cute anyway."

"She will be cute. All newborns are."

"If you say so."

They came to Kyle and Joyce's room, and Rex paused outside the door, ready to lie, it seemed, to fuss over a child that he feared would be homely.

Not a chance, not if the parents had anything to do with it. As soon as they went inside, Lisa caught sight of the Prescotts. Joyce, a strong-boned, striking blonde was sitting up in bed, drinking orange juice and gazing at her husband and daughter. She looked over at Lisa and Rex and smiled.

Kyle was seated beside the crib, staring at the sleeping baby, and when he stood to greet them, Lisa nearly gulped. He was at least six feet four of raw, rugged muscle. He wore his shoulder-length hair in a straight, blunt cut. He looked like a warrior.

Hugs and handshakes were exchanged, introductions were made and gifts were dispersed.

"Daniel and Allie aren't here yet," Kyle said, directing them to his daughter.

"We're a little early," Rex responded.

Lisa gazed at the baby. Patricia Ann Prescott looked like an angel, with a tuft of brown hair and chubby cheeks. Her medium-tone skin defined her mixed-blood heritage. Lisa realized that the child she was carrying had the same genetics: one quarter Native and three-quarters Anglo.

"Wow." Rex seemed truly awed. "She's beautiful. Look how tiny her hands are."

"Want to hold her?" the proud Papa asked.

"Me?" Now Rex seemed to panic. "I don't—"

"Don't worry, bro, you won't break her." Kyle reached for the newborn and winked at Lisa.

Patricia stirred in her daddy's arms, and he transferred the tiny bundle to Rex, who lowered himself into a chair and treated her like glass.

He looked good with a baby, Lisa thought. Terrified, but good.

The little girl made a squeaking sound, and he glanced up. "What do I do if she cries?"

"Worse yet, what do you do if she poops?" Kyle laughed. "You're doing fine. Don't worry about it."

"Listen to my husband." Joyce laughed, too. "He changed his first dirty diaper today. Now he's a pro."

Rex looked at Lisa, and they shared a smile. He was starting to rock the baby. Patricia quit squeaking and went back to sleep.

"You need to hold her, too," Kyle said to Lisa.

"I'd love to."

Soon the baby was settled into her arms, and she felt an instant connection. Motherhood was in her blood.

No, she thought. It wasn't. Not if Maggie was her biological mom.

Kyle put a pacifier into his daughter's rosebud mouth, and she suckled. Lisa held her even closer.

Allie and Daniel arrived, also bearing gifts. Once again, kisses and hugs were exchanged, and Lisa was quickly introduced to the other couple. Kyle was eager for them to hold Patricia, insisting they have a turn.

Daniel, a square-jawed guy with full-blood features, looked even more terrified than Rex had been, causing Rex to give him advice.

"How quickly they learn," Joyce said, marveling at the men.

Lisa nodded and smiled. She stood next to Allie, who was tall and trim with straight dark hair that fell to her waist. She wore gypsy clothes and lots of jewelry. On her left hand was an engagement ring.

She was different than Lisa had pictured. Prettier, softer, more relaxed. No one would ever suspect that her mother was a cold-blooded killer, not if they didn't already know the truth. Allie had what appeared to be a gentle heart. Lisa felt an emotional kinship toward her, especially when Allie took her hand and gave it an encouraging squeeze.

By the time Allie held the baby and did it quite naturally, Kyle was doling out pink-banded cigars to the men. Basking in baby success, they tucked them into their pockets.

Finally Patricia was given to her mother, and the lady cop cradled her perfect daughter.

"Olivia is coming by," Kyle said to Lisa and Rex. "She's flying in from D.C. and will be here around noon. She told us we were having a girl before we were even pregnant. I'll bet she'll know if you're having a boy or a girl."

"Who is she?" Lisa asked.

"Olivia is my sister," Allie answered. "She's psychic. She's not always right. No psychic is. But she's highly gifted and good at what she does. She works with the police and the FBI. She's married to a special agent. He was the profiler on our mother's case, and Joyce was one of the lead detectives."

"Maybe she'll be able to give you a reading about what's happening to you," Daniel said, clearly referring to the threats.

"Maybe," Rex responded, sounding hopeful. "I haven't seen Olivia in years." He turned to Lisa. "She used to date Kyle."

"But it was never serious," Allie added. She looked at Rex. "Funny that you and I only met recently. You'd think our paths would have crossed sooner." She shifted her gaze to Lisa. "He did the investigative work on my stalking."

"Yes, he told me about it. I'm sorry that someone tried to hurt you."

"And I'm sorry someone is trying to hurt you."

After a beat of silence, Kyle said, "Ian is coming with Olivia. He might be able to help, too."

Lisa assumed Ian was the FBI husband.

Another bout of silence ensued, a reminder that this was supposed to be a happy occasion, not a catch-the-bad-guys gathering.

The conversation turned to a lighthearted topic, but Lisa couldn't get the psychic or the profiler out of her mind. Apparently neither could Rex.

He kept glancing at his watch, anxious for them to arrive.

## Chapter 12

Olivia and her husband showed up just after noon. For Rex, it was strange to see Olivia married and settled. He'd always considered her a completely independent woman. She still was, he supposed, to some degree. Luckily, Ian, or Agent West as he was known in the FBI realm, complemented his wife.

He was a Muscogee Creek mixed-blood with mostly Anglo roots. He was originally from Oklahoma and had the oddest gray eyes Rex had ever seen. When the light hit them they turned silver. Olivia was her usual sleek, slim, tight-black-clothes, choppy-haired self.

Lisa seemed impressed with both of them. Or maybe it was a curious sense of awe, as they were a compelling couple.

Rex waited until they got some quality time with everyone before he let them know that he needed their help, and they agreed to meet with him and Lisa in the lobby after the baby visit ended.

So here they were, just the four of them, discussing the troubling events taking place in Rex and Lisa's lives.

Ian, the profiler, listened to details about the case and the suspected perpetrators. From the information provided to him, he agreed that the analysis Rex and the LAPD had made of Tim and Maggie seemed accurate.

"They very well could be Lisa's biological parents," he said. "It certainly strengthens their motive, the possessiveness and anger directed toward her."

"I don't know," his wife put in, making all of them turn in her direction.

Olivia was an empath, a psychic who had the ability to scan people's minds, tapping into thoughts and feelings. She also had visions, sometimes clear, sometimes distorted, of past, present and future occurrences.

"You don't know what?" Rex asked. "That Maggie and Tim are the perpetrators or that they're Lisa's parents."

"That they're her parents." Olivia ran her hand through her hair, spiking the shiny dark layers. Her eyes were heavily lined, enhancing her mystic appearance. "I just don't feel it. Not in that sense."

"Then what do you feel?" Lisa wanted to know. Up until now, she'd been quiet, taking everything in.

"It's as if you belonged to them, yet you didn't. I can't quite explain it nor do I know what it means. It's a bit mixed up in my mind."

Her husband cocked his head. "Are you feeling anything else?"

"No." She divided her gaze between Lisa and Rex. "I'm sorry."

"It's okay," Lisa responded. "Maybe it will make sense to us later."

"It usually does," Ian said of his wife's ability. To Rex he added, "If the DNA tests are negative, then maybe you should research the adoption. There could still be a link."

"I agree and I will." But Rex hoped that he wasn't running out of time. "How long do you think it'll be before Maggie and Tim quit making threats and act on them? Do you think they're waiting to see if Lisa gets frightened enough to have an abortion? Or gets stressed enough to miscarry?"

"Yes, but I doubt they'll wait past the first trimester," the profiler said. "After twelve weeks abortions are more complicated and miscarriages are far less likely."

Lisa drew a ragged breath and Rex put his hand on her knee. They were already over halfway through the first trimester.

"I won't let them hurt you or the baby." He repeated what he'd told her so many times before.

"I know," she said. But knowing didn't lessen the fear in her eyes.

No one spoke for what seemed like a full minute, a long time if you're just sitting there looking at each other.

Then Olivia leaned toward Lisa and Rex, and he suspected that she'd just gotten a feeling, only it didn't seem bad.

"What's going on?" Rex asked.

She smiled a little. "Do you want to know what the baby is?"

A future-daddy moment punched him warmly in the gut. He glanced at Lisa, and their gazes locked. It was too early for an ultrasound to give them that information.

"I want to know," he said to her. "Do you?"

She nodded and sat more forward in her chair. The lobby was unoccupied, with the exception of the four of them. Five, if you included the life in her womb.

"It's a girl," Olivia said.

Lisa reacted by cradling the daughter inside her, and Rex said, *"Kamama"* and got the urge to go back and hold Kyle and Joyce's baby again.

The psychic looked at Rex. "Butterfly?"

He doubted that Olivia spoke Cherokee. She was from the Chiricahua Apache and Lakota Sioux Nations. Mostly likely she'd picked up on the translation from his mind.

"It's our nickname for a girl."

"That's sweet. A little flutter bug."

"Yeah." He took Lisa's hand and held it. She seemed to be feeling better now, less afraid.

"Olivia has never been wrong with a baby prediction," Ian said, smiling at his woman.

"Then maybe we should start buying pink stuff." Rex thought about the future nursery at Lisa's house. It was already decorated in pastels; they had a jump start.

"Not all girls like pink," Olivia teased, indicating her black garb.

"Ours will," Rex assured her. Their daughter was going to be made of sugar and spice and everything nice. That old saying fit.

More baby talk ensued, making their conversation easy and comfortable.

But not for long.

Soon Olivia grabbed Ian's arm and shuddered. Something was happening in her mind....

Something awful.

Ian watched his wife with dreadful concern, and Rex prayed that she wasn't seeing broken butterflies. By now, Lisa was squeezing his hand as tightly as the psychic was holding on to her husband.

"They died," Olivia said suddenly. "In a bombing."

"Who?" the profiler asked, before Rex could speak. "Who died?"

"People connected to Lisa." Olivia came out of her trance, breathing heavily. "All I saw was the explosion. I couldn't tell what building it was or what the people looked like."

Rex got his voice back. "But you know that they were connected to Lisa?"

"It happened when she was a baby. You need to find out more." Olivia turned to her husband. "And you need to help him."

"Absolutely," the special agent responded. Then to Lisa he asked, "How old are you?"

"Thirty," she told him.

Ian gazed at Rex with his odd gray eyes. "We'll

start with white supremacist bombings from thirty years ago."

That sounded logical, but whether it was accurate remained to be seen. Lisa looked as if she didn't know what to think, and Rex understood. Olivia's vision created yet another puzzle.

Rex and Ian agreed to get started right away, and later that night, after extensive hours of research, clouds brewed in the sky, bringing unexpected weather to an already complicated day.

While rain slashed against the windows, Rex climbed into bed with Lisa. He got under the covers but didn't turn out the light. He suspected that she would want to talk for a while.

She did, asking him, "Did you come across anything that seems pertinent?"

"At this point, it's tough to tell. We've got a lot of material to analyze."

Although the special agent was an unofficial investigator on the case, his FBI resources were likely to speed up the process.

"You look tired, Rex."

"I am." So was the profiler. He'd left about twenty minutes ago. "But I'm not too tired to stay up with you."

"I've been trying to sleep, but I can't." She angled

her body more toward his, adjusting the straps on her nightgown. "I keep thinking about everything. Do you think it's possible that Tim and Maggie are responsible for the bombing? That they killed people who were close to me?" Before he could answer, she added, "Maybe it was my birth parents who died. Maybe the bombing made me an orphan and that's why Tim and Maggie have been following me around."

"What for? Out of guilt?"

"Yes. And in their twisted minds, they became my surrogate family. That would explain Olivia's comment about me belonging to them, yet not belonging to them." She clutched the top of the blanket, reacting, it seemed, to the weather. Rain was still hitting the windows. "Olivia doesn't think Tim and Maggie are my parents and neither do I."

"Olivia said she was mixed up about that part of the reading," he reminded her.

"I know, but I'm not. I'm certain that my birth parents were good people."

"I'm glad you feel that way, but it could still turn out to be Maggie and Tim." He skimmed the side of her jaw, tracing the angles of her face. Every time he was this close to her, her features became more and more familiar. "Either way, we should know by tomorrow or the next day. The results should be in by then."

"It's going to be a long wait."

"Try not to think about it." He lowered his hand to her stomach. "Just relax and take care of our daughter."

"You believe that it's a girl?"

He nodded. "Don't you?"

"Yes. But I also believe that she isn't Maggie and Tim's grandchild."

He wasn't going to argue with her, but he wasn't going to agree with what she hoped was or wasn't true. He gestured to the window and changed the subject. "In Cherokee mythology, there are two kinds of Thunder Beings. Those who live close to the earth and those who bring blessings of rain to the people."

She managed a smile. "Then it looks as if we're being blessed."

"We are." And he was grateful that he'd taken her mind off Maggie and Tim. He leaned over to kiss her, and she nuzzled closer.

Mouth to mouth, they connected. He lowered the blanket and lifted the hem of her nightgown, slipping his hand between her legs. She wasn't wearing panties.

She sighed, and he did his best to please her. He used his fingers, rubbing her most intimate place and making her moist. She slid the top of her night-gown down and pressed against him, her breasts to his chest.

He kept touching her, and she got wetter and wetter.

After she came, he brought his fingers to her lips and offered her a taste. She obligated him naughtily.

He watched her, and soon she tugged at his sweatpants until he had no choice but to remove them. Her nightgown came off, too.

Naked, they embraced, filled with the want of each other. Tumbling over the bed, she ended up on her hands and knees, and he got behind her.

Would he ever stop wanting her? He didn't think so, and being this hungry for her scared him.

But not enough to stop. He penetrated her, hotly, deeply, taking what he needed.

Rex slid his hands around her waist and wondered if this would be their position of choice later, after her tummy swelled.

She arched her body, inviting him to thrust harder. Somehow they managed to turn their heads enough to kiss, only it was a rough, almost biting motion. He would've let her draw blood if it suited her. By now, she was guiding one of his hands lower, down her stomach and between her legs, so he could rub her again.

Greedy girl.

He continued to move inside her, and the lust-driven rhythm intensified.

Desperate man.

They climaxed together in a state of mindless arousal, the slick-sweated heat of their joining as powerful as the Thunder Beings who'd brought the rain.

The sun shone the next day, and Lisa wondered if last night had been a dream. Only she knew it wasn't.

Rex and Ian were working at her house once again, taking over the living room and continuing the bombing research. She hoped they figured it out. If not, it would only be one more thing to worry about.

She sat at the dining table, sipping mint tea and eating peach cobbler. Thank goodness it was afternoon. Mornings were still rough on her, as the pregnancy sickness had yet to pass.

The doorbell rang, and she hopped up. Maybe it was Olivia. Ian's wife was supposed to stop by later.

"I'll get it," she said, and breezed past the men.

She flung open the door and found Cathy, her former employee, on the other side. The Snow White girl flashed a let-bygones-be-bygones smile. As always, she had a headband in her hair, and in her arms was the cutest, fluffiest little pup.

They came inside, and Cathy said, "This is Barker," and extended the Chipoo like a peace offering.

"Oh, he's an angel." Lisa took him and brought him up to her face. He wiggled and gave her a wet kiss, right on the tip of her nose.

Cathy noticed Rex, and he caught sight of her, too. He raised his eyebrows at Lisa in an "I told you so" manner, indicating his prediction that Cathy would return with her feelings intact.

He greeted the brunette and introduced Ian as Special Agent West. Cathy made an "Oh" with her mouth, impressed that the FBI was there.

The women went to the kitchen with Barker in tow, and Lisa got her guest some cobbler and tea.

"Things must be heating up," Cathy said.

"They are. It's been crazy." While they ate, Barker curled up on Lisa's lap. "I'm so glad you're here. I haven't filled your position at the studio yet. You can have your job back if you want it."

"Oh, that's great. I was hoping I could come back. Nelson isn't mad anymore, either. He agreed that we should try to support you through this."

"Thank you. I'm so sorry for the way we treated you guys."

Cathy waved her fork. "You've already apologized enough. Are there any leads? Do you know who's been threatening you?"

"Yes, but we don't have enough proof."

"That sucks. Is it anyone I know?"

"No." And even if it were, Lisa wouldn't have named names. "I just want it to end."

"If there's anything you need, just let me know."

Lisa smiled. "Maybe I could keep Barker."

The pup's mistress shook her head, but she was smiling, too. "Anything but that. He's my baby."

And Lisa's baby was in her tummy. Her daughter. Her butterfly.

Cathy stayed for about an hour, saying goodbye to Rex and the special agent on her way out.

Afterward, Lisa lingered in the living room, watching them work. Between their laptops, the fax machine they'd set up and the calls they were making, she assumed that they were collecting vital information.

Rather than poke her nose into it, she asked, "Is anyone hungry? I'd be glad to fix lunch." Besides needing a balanced meal herself, she was anxious for something to do. The studio was closed today. She had nothing but time on her hands.

Ian answered first. "Sure. That sounds great."

"Me, too," Rex added.

"Are enchiladas all right?" she asked.

"Fine," said Ian, without glancing up.

"Same here," responded an equally preoccupied Rex.

Retreating to her task, Lisa cleared the cobbler dishes from the table and got cracking on lunch.

While the beef and onions browned, she grated cheese and got the ingredients ready for Spanish rice.

Halfway through the preparation, the doorbell sounded and she assumed it was Olivia, maybe even Allie and Daniel, too. Not a problem, she thought. There would be plenty of food for all of them. Lisa was making a big pan of enchiladas. She tended to cook more than enough, but she enjoyed leftovers.

Since she had her hands full, she didn't rush to answer the summons. Instead she let Rex get the door.

A minute or so later when he entered the kitchen alone with a serious expression, she was confused.

"What's going on?" she asked.

"It was a delivery." He held out a sealed envelope. "From the lab."

"Oh, my God. The results of the test." Her hands started to shake. "Will you open it?"

He nodded and tore the flap. As he lifted a white sheet of paper, her pulse pounded at her throat.

He read it, and she waited for his response, praying that Maggie and Tim weren't her parents.

He looked up, and her pulse pounded again.

"Not a biological match," he said.

Her knees went weak with relief. But her relief didn't last long.

By the end of the week, Ian and Rex uncovered details about the bombing and discovered who her birth parents actually were, and it was worse than she could've imagined.

## Chapter 13

Lisa struggled to comprehend the truth, to accept it. She and Rex were at a nearby park, where they'd gone to discuss the details. The bright and sunny setting did little to ease the tension.

She could have been in the depths of hell.

Her birth parents' names were John and Denise Masterson. They were white supremacists.

They were also murderers.

When Lisa was only two months old, John and Denise had bombed a cultural center in Los Angeles. At the time, the center was hosting a family gathering for ethnic minorities. It had been one of the worst cases of racial violence the city had ever seen—a massacre of men, women and children.

She glanced at Rex. They sat near the pond, but they weren't feeding the ducks. Rex claimed it was bad for the environment and for the life cycle of the birds.

"Are you sure they're my parents?" she asked.

"Yes. We obtained a copy of the adoption records."

Of course they did, she thought. A private investigator and an off-the-clock special agent would do no less.

"I'm sorry, Lisa."

"At least they're dead." During the course of the bombing, John and Denise had gotten too close to the explosion, killing themselves along with their victims.

"There's a bit more I need to tell you."

She braced herself. "Go ahead."

"We discovered that Maggie and Tim are your godparents, and after John and Denise died, they tried to adopt you. But they were denied."

That explained why they'd gotten so possessive of her. She rubbed her arms, chilled, even if it was a warm day. "Were they denied because of their association with the bombers?"

He nodded. "The adoption agency was concerned that they'd been involved, too."

"Do you think they were?"

"Yes, but there was never any evidence linking them to the crime. They were questioned, along with other members of their organization, but no charges were ever filed."

"Which is probably what's making them so bold now," she said. "The reason they think they can get away with threatening me. What does Bell think about all of this?"

"He considers them suspects. But he still doesn't have any evidence against them."

"So there isn't anything the police can do, other than question Tim and Maggie when they drift in from their phony vacation?"

"If I could get away with threatening them right back, I would."

"Vigilantism is illegal."

"So is what they're doing to you. Better me being in the line of fire than a woman and child."

Because it seemed useless to argue, she turned quiet. In the silence, he sat back and watched the ducks.

Lisa followed the birds, too. Some were light, some were dark and some were a combination of both, all cohabitating together. "Was I baptized at the church Tim and Maggie attend?"

"Yes, but it had a different name then."

"Did you come across any pictures of John and Denise?"

He turned away from the pond. "You don't want to see them, do you?"

There was a part of her that wanted to know what they looked like and another part that was afraid of seeing herself in their faces. "Maybe. I don't know."

"I don't think it's a good idea."

Of course he didn't. He was trying to protect her. "I favor them, don't I?"

He didn't respond right away. Was he debating if he should lie? "A little," he finally said.

A lot, she thought. He'd downplayed the truth. "I'm not like them inside." She wrapped her arms around her knees. She'd wanted so badly to believe that her birth parents had been decent people. "How could they kill innocent families? Children?"

"Don't think about it, Lisa."

Sage advice that never seemed to work. "I should visit the victims' graves. I should bring them flowers." And tell them how sorry she was. "Do you have their names? Can you find out what cemeteries they're at?"

He nodded. "But I don't want you going alone. We'll arrange some time to go together."

"Thank you." There was no way to right the wrong, but at least she could try.

With the father of her baby by her side.

* * *

It was harder than Lisa imagined. For three days, she and Rex drove from cemetery to cemetery, with a list of the bombing victims and the location of their graves.

This was the final day, the final cemetery and the final family on their list. It was quiet, unlike yesterday's experience, where a funeral procession and casket-lowering had taken place, crowding the burial grounds.

Today's stillness gave her no peace. The serenity of grassy slopes and carefully chosen headstones made her terribly sad.

Fearful, too. Was death dark? Was it lonely? How had it been for the people her birth parents had killed? Quick? Chaotic? Were they panic-stricken? Had they suffered before they'd died or had the explosion taken them instantly? Had children clung to their mothers? Had husbands reached for their wives only to have parts of their bodies blown to bits?

Families, she thought. Human lives destroyed in the blink of an eye.

As they walked toward the resting places of Esteban, Mary and Manny Alvarez, her breath hitched. Manny had been only two years old when he'd died.

"Do you think my parents are going to start feeling differently about me now?" She and Rex had told her mom and dad the whole sordid story, and although they'd reacted like the caring, supportive family they'd always been, she still worried about the long-term effect.

He stopped walking, and they stood at the top of a hill with a sea of graves around them. "How can you say that? How can you even think it? Your mom and dad love you."

"I know. But it almost makes adoption seem like a crap shoot. You never really know what you're getting."

"Your parents got a beautiful baby who grew into a beautiful young woman."

Then why did she feel so dirty, so tainted? When Rex leaned over to give her a gentle kiss, she almost pulled away. As she stiffened, he whispered an endearment against her lips.

For all the good it did. At the moment, she didn't feel as if she deserved it.

Much too emotional, she clutched the gifts in her hand. Flowers for Esteban and Mary and a Winnie the Pooh pinwheel for Manny.

Tears collected in her eyes. Was it Rex's affection or sorrow for the dead that was making her cry?

He stepped back, and she sniffed and put on a

brave smile that made her ache in the center of her mixed-up soul.

"I'll be okay," she told him.

He didn't look as if he believed her, but he kept quiet.

When they reached the Alvarezes' grave site, she knelt to put the gifts in place. Had they been identified by their dental records? The thought made her sick.

"Manny would have been thirty-two by now," she said. "Probably married with kids of his own."

"It's called survivor's guilt, Lisa."

"What is?"

"What you're feeling."

"How can it be survivor's guilt? I wasn't there when it happened."

"No, but you feel responsible. If John and Denise would have brought you with them that day, you would have perished with them and everyone else."

"I'm glad John and Denise are dead." She adjusted the pinwheel, hoping it would spin, but it didn't. "You're right, though. I do feel guilty about the innocent people who were taken." Manny's little grave had a teddy bear etched on it.

"Maybe you should talk to someone."

"I am talking to someone. I'm talking to you."

She looked into his eyes. She'd been telling herself that she was half in love with him, but that was a lie. She was all the way in love, and between what she felt for him and what she'd learned about her birth parents, she wanted to curl up in a ball and hide from the world.

Could she feel any worse? Her genetics haunted the very core of her, and she loved a man who didn't love her back. No strings attached except for the baby. He was still living by that motto. So was she, only in pretense.

"I don't think I'm equipped to fix this for you," he said.

He was talking about her survivor's guilt. She wondered what he would say if she admitted that she loved him. It didn't matter because she wouldn't dare tell him that she'd gone and done the unthinkable.

"I'll get through it on my own," she responded.

"Will you?"

"I'm going to try."

"At least talk to your mom and dad."

Once again, he was referring to the guilt. But he was probably referring to her fears about the adoption, too.

She couldn't deny his advice. She needed reassurance that her parents still loved her. Although deep down she knew they did, she needed to hear them say it out loud.

"How did you get so wise?" she asked.

He smiled, then shrugged, then frowned. "I'm not very wise about my own life. I still haven't told my mom and dad about our daughter."

Because he couldn't handle their reaction, she thought. The old-fashioned pressure they would put on him to marry her.

"You'll tell them when you're ready," she responded for lack of something better to say.

"Yeah, but when will that be? After the threats are over? After Tim and Maggie are in prison? Or will I wait until *Kamama* is born?"

"I don't know." But him calling the baby by her nickname made Lisa's heart tighten in her chest.

"I guess we're both not thinking clearly today. Sometimes life gets confusing."

"So does death." She gazed at the granite markers in front of them. "Do you speak Spanish?"

"No. Why? Did you want to say a prayer for Manny and his parents in Spanish?"

She nodded. Spanish was the Alvarezes' native tongue.

"I know the Lord's Prayer in Cherokee. Would that be all right? I can teach it to you. A gift from our child to theirs."

She cradled her stomach, anxious for the little one to grow, to move about, to flutter its butterfly wings. "I think that's a beautiful idea."

"I'll say a verse, then you can repeat it."

"Okay." She remained on her knees and so did he.

The language was difficult for Lisa to enunciate, but she recited the words the best she could, saying each one carefully.

As Rex reached for her hand, offering his support, the pinwheel began to move, turning slowly, making the soft, spring breeze part of the prayer.

She hoped it was a sign that Manny and his parents were actually listening.

The next day, Rex took Lisa to her parents' house. Dad was on a vintage car excursion with Grandpa, but Mom was available.

"I'm going to take off," Rex said. "Call me when you want me to come back and get you."

"I can bring her home," Mom said.

"Okay. Thanks." He turned to Lisa. "But I still want you to call me."

"I will." She had to work later, but for now she was hanging on to what was left of her emotional sanity. "Where are you going?"

"To my place to catch up on a few things."

An icy sensation shot through her blood. The

last time he'd returned to his condo, the gutted rabbit had been waiting for him on his doorstep.

He gauged her expression, as if reading her mind. "I can stay here if you'd prefer. I don't have to go right now."

"That's okay." Rex had set up security cameras around his condo. He'd done the same thing around her house, from all angles. If Tim and Maggie or anyone else crept onto either property, their images would be on film.

"You sure? I don't mind staying."

"No, really, it's all right. You should go." She needed some time alone with her mom.

Who, by the way, was watching Lisa and Rex with a curious eye. Self-conscious, they didn't hug or kiss. They merely said goodbye.

Except…

As he headed for the door, he glanced back, making her want to rush into his arms. But holding on to him wasn't going to keep her safe, at least not from loving him.

She was too far gone for that.

He left, and Mom said, "You fell for him, didn't you?"

Lisa nodded. By now, her knees were shaky. She sat on the sofa and drew her legs up. "Everything is out of control. The way I feel about him, the way I'm afraid you and Dad might start feeling about me."

"Me and Dad? What are you talking about?"

"The adoption, Mom, and who my birth parents are."

"Oh, dear heaven." The older woman sat beside her. "You can't possibly think that would ever affect how your father and I feel about you. You're our baby, our perfect little girl. Nothing could ever change that. Nothing ever will. We could *never, ever* love you any less."

"But what if you knew then what you know now? Would you have adopted me anyway?"

"Yes. Absolutely." Maternal love. Maternal compassion. "You were an innocent child. Nothing that those people did has anything to do with you."

Needing to get closer, Lisa put her head on her mom's lap. As always, Mom looked like the warmhearted, family-oriented suburban lady she was. When Lisa was little, she used to think that her mom could've been in a Kool-Aid commercial. "Rex says I have survivor's guilt."

A gentle hand stroked her hair. "Rex seems to know you pretty well."

"Not well enough."

"He doesn't suspect that you love him?"

"We agreed to a no-strings relationship."

"Then maybe you should—"

"Tell him how I feel?" She sat up, her heart racing. "I can't. It would freak him out. He isn't a commitment kind of guy."

"So you're just going to suffer through it?"

"I'd be suffering more if I told him. Besides, I knew better. Even you warned me not to get too attached."

"I shouldn't have said anything. That wasn't my place."

"Yes, it was. If my daughter was in danger of falling for the wrong man, I'd tell her, too."

Mom poked Lisa's tummy. "It could be a boy."

"No. No. Didn't I tell you? Olivia said it was a girl, and Rex and I are sure it is, too."

Mom grinned. "You're all psychics now?"

"I guess so." She grinned, too, feeling a bit better.

"You know what we should do? We should go out and look at baby furniture. We should start designing your nursery."

"It sounds fun, but this early?"

"We don't have to buy anything. We're just going to get some ideas."

"Okay." Now she really did feel better. But that was what moms were for. Lisa got off the couch, ready to window shop.

Then a moment of fear set in, like the quiet before the storm. But she willed it away, refusing to create an obstacle in her mind.

## Chapter 14

Rex's cell phone rang, and seeing Lisa's name on the screen made his pulse jump, which wasn't a good thing. For him, it was totally out of character, and he didn't like it.

He'd been thinking about her all day, not the case, not the baby, but *her,* and being consumed by a woman preyed on emotions he didn't know he had. The distant way they'd said goodbye earlier had left him feeling empty. Distracted, too. He'd barely gotten anything done.

The phone chimed again, and he cursed to himself and answered it. He was way too anxious to hear her voice.

"Rex?" she said, after he said "Hello."

"Yeah, it's me."

"You sound different."

"I'm the same." Or so he hoped. "Where are you?"

"In my mom's car. We're headed to my house. Where are you?"

"I'm still at the condo." And it seemed vacant, even though it was packed with his belongings. Maybe he'd just been away for too long. Maybe he just needed to get used to it again.

Her voice bubbled, girlish and happy. "Guess where we went? Looking at baby furniture. It was so much fun. I found the most adorable crib set."

He wasn't sure what a crib set was, but he assumed it was the bedding.

She continued. "It's called butterfly magic. Isn't that perfect? There's even a matching lamp and mobile that goes with it."

"So, you bought it?"

"No. I'm going to get it later. I need to decide what type of crib to get first. There's still plenty of time." She paused and her voice changed. Less confident, less excited. "Is a butterfly set okay with you? You don't think it's too much, do you? Calling her butterfly and putting butterflies in her room?"

"No, of course not. *Kamama* will love it." He didn't know anything about decorating a nursery, but he cared about how the room looked. He'd already considered the color scheme. "Is the set pink or pastel or whatever?"

"It's mostly pink, but it has other colors in it, too. It's a quilted design." Lisa sounded happy again. "I can show it to you online."

"Sure. That sounds great. I'll be headed home soon, too." *Home?* It was bad enough that he couldn't get her off his mind. He didn't need to get attached to her house, too. The place was too damn small for him, too damn feminine. He had his own digs.

"Oh, no," she said. "My phone is starting to beep. It's going to go dead."

"Call me back on your mom's cell." He didn't want to lose the connection, not just yet.

"I can't. She didn't bring her phone. I'll see you at home."

*Home.* She'd said it, too. But it was her home. It made sense coming from her.

They hung up, and he gave himself about thirty minutes to clear his head before he left his condo and got in his car. But he didn't leave the parking lot. He sat there for another minute or two. Anxious, he considered calling Lisa at her house, but he refrained.

Besides, she might not even be there yet. She hadn't told him where they'd gone to look at baby goods. At this hour, they could've hit traffic.

Finally, he started his engine and took off.

Halfway there, his phone rang. Foolishly, he hoped it was Lisa. It wasn't. He checked the screen. The caller was Special Agent West, who was back in Virginia where he and his wife lived.

Rex pushed the hands-free button. "Ian?" He assumed the other man had come across some information. "What's up?"

"It's Olivia. She just got this strange feeling, and I wanted to check on you and Lisa. Is everything all right?"

"Strange in what way?" Was Olivia sensing the discord in his emotions? Was this a personal call?

"Did you and Lisa visit the bombing victims' graves?"

His heart slammed his rib cage. "Yes. Why?"

"That's part of the feeling Olivia got. She thinks that Tim and Maggie saw you at one of the cemeteries. That they followed you. Is that possible? Could they have been nearby and gone unnoticed?"

"There was a burial the second day. Lots of cars. Lots of people. It didn't even dawn on me that…" The heart slamming continued. "What else is Olivia feeling?"

"That they're angry that you brought gifts to the victims. She thinks today might be the day."

"For them to act on the threats? Oh, God. I have to go. I have to call Lisa. She's on her way home."

"Tell her to stay there. No, wait." A woman's voice sounded in the background. "Olivia said for her not to stay there. If something happens, it's going to be at Lisa's house. Did you hear me? Don't let her stay there."

"Yes, I heard you."

Edgy, Rex ended the call and dialed Lisa's landline. Her voice mail answered. He left a frantic message. His mind was spinning like a disoriented top. He was speeding, too, changing lanes, trying to fight the traffic and make it to Lisa's house in time.

In time for what?

What did Tim and Maggie have planned? What were they going to do?

He called Detective Bell and got his voice mail, too. Where the hell was everyone? He left a message for the cop, telling him that he'd gotten a tip that something was going to happen at Lisa's house. He didn't mention that it had been a psychic tip. He doubted that Bell would have taken him seriously. Bell was the practical sort.

Maybe Olivia was wrong. Maybe this wasn't the day.

Lord, he hoped not. He'd never been so ill-prepared. All this time he'd been staying close to

Lisa, and now she'd fallen out of his grasp. He called her landline again and got the voice mail. He left a second message.

Was she there? Were she and her mom having a snack on the porch and unable to hear the phone?

He finally made it to Lisa's neighborhood and when he attempted to turn onto her street, he was unable to proceed. Two cars had collided and were blocking his path. There wasn't enough room to get around them. It looked like a fender bender to him, but the drivers, two grumpy old women, weren't budging. They were arguing in the road.

He rolled down his window and yelled at them. "Move your cars!"

The older of the two rounded on him. "We're waiting for the police to arrive to take a report."

He didn't tell them that he'd called the cops, too. "You can still move out of the way."

"Not a chance," she said. "I want them to see how the accident occurred. That she hit me when I was trying to turn into my driveway."

He didn't need this. Not now. He was tempted to push them out of the way, but he pulled over and jammed his car into Park, leaving it at the curb.

The women looked at him as if he were mad.

He was. He started running toward Lisa's house,

and not knowing what to expect put him in a panic, fear-drenched adrenaline slamming through his veins.

Lisa's house came into view and he saw her mom's car parked in the driveway.

He never made it to the door. The unexpected hit first.

The front of the house exploded in a sudden and violent burst. The pressure propelled him backward, even as he tried so desperately to keep running, to reach them, to save them.

Debris flew toward him, and he landed on the ground in a shower of glass and wood.

Tears rushed his eyes. He could hear chaos all around him. People running out of their houses. Voices screaming.

He looked up through the haze. The back portion of the house was still standing, and although the car in the driveway was covered in debris, it hadn't exploded.

Were they still alive? Rex climbed to his feet and ran toward the ruins, mindless of his injuries.

He tore through the wreckage, calling their names, but no one answered. He couldn't find Lisa or her mother.

Sirens shrilled in the background. Help was on its way, but Rex wasn't going to stop searching. There was a lot of rubble, a lot places they could be.

Dead or alive.

Time passed, but he had no concept of it. Was it seconds? Minutes? He stumbled over what appeared to be one of Lisa's shoes. A red high heel. He picked it up and held it achingly against his chest.

A masculine voice sounded behind him. "Son, I think you should come with me. What if there's another bomb set to go off?"

Rex spun around. He didn't recognize the man. He was short and round with graying hair. He didn't behave like a plain-clothes cop, and he wasn't wearing an ATF vest or fireman gear. He was probably someone who lived nearby and saw Rex run into the shattered building.

"I don't care if there's another bomb." Rex couldn't think beyond Lisa's survival. "I need to find the woman who lives here. Her and her mother."

"Lisa and Rita Gordon are safe. They were at my house when the bomb went off. My wife invited them over to pick lemons. We have a tree that—"

Rex didn't listen to the rest. "Where are they now?"

"Outside. Lisa's hysterical. Especially when I told her that a young man was here. She wanted to come after you, but her mother wouldn't let her." The neighbor looked around, anxious for the authorities to arrive. He didn't like playing the hero. "Can we go now?"

Hell, yes.

They left the wreckage and dashed into the sun. Rex scanned the crowd that had gathered.

"I don't see her." His heart was pounding so hard it sounded like a drum in his ears.

"Over there." The man pointed.

Rex turned, and Lisa broke free of her mom's hold and ran toward him. He ran, too, until they were locked in a tight embrace.

A throng of emergency vehicles arrived. Cops controlled the crowd, and a bomb squad headed for the house. Rex and Lisa ignored everyone but each other.

He spoke first. "I was so afraid you were…"

She gazed up at him. Watery streaks lined her pretty face. She was shaking in his arms. "Look at you. You're hurt."

"It's nothing." Cuts and bruises, tiny shards of glass under his skin, but he didn't care. All that mattered was keeping her close, keeping her safe.

"They destroyed my house." She kept shaking. "Did they even care who they might've killed?"

He told her about Ian's call. "Olivia said they were angry because they knew we went to the grave sites. I guess it didn't matter to them if you were in the house nor not. Either way, they made their point."

"What about next time?"

"There isn't going to be another time." He reminded her about the hidden cameras. The units closest to the house would be gone, but not the one from across the street. "Whoever set the bomb will be on tape. The police will have the evidence they need to arrest them."

She put her head on his shoulder. "Almost everything I own is gone. What am I going to do?"

"Move in with me," he responded instantly.

Lisa lifted her head. "It would be better for me to go to my parents' house."

"No, it wouldn't. You belong with me. I'll take care of you. We can get married."

She went still, frozen like a statue, staring at him as if he were crazy. Maybe he was. He hadn't expected to propose. Not now. Not ever. But he'd said the words, and he didn't want to take them back.

"You don't really mean it," she said. "You're reacting out of fear. You'll regret it later."

"Why would I regret it? You're having my baby. People who have kids should be married."

"People in love should be married." She stepped back, hugging herself instead of letting him embrace her.

"We can still have a good life together."

She disagreed. "That makes no sense."

Yes, it did. Didn't it? By now, he was confused and his injuries were starting to hurt. He didn't know anything about being in love, but neither did she. He wanted to pour some sense into her. Having a baby should be enough.

Fresh tears collected in her makeup-smeared eyes. "I think I should go to my parents' house now."

"The police are going to want to interview us."

"Then afterward."

"I'll go with you."

"No, Rex. You should get some medical attention, then go to your own house. This is too much for us right now."

"Don't shut me out." What in God's name was he going to do without her, without the baby?

"We can talk later. I can call you tonight."

He couldn't believe this was happening. Her house blew up, right along with their relationship. "How am I supposed to protect you if we're not together?"

"You just said that Tim and Maggie will get caught."

"They will, but you still need me to keep you safe."

"I'll stay close to my parents. Besides, you've got cameras at their house, too."

Her logic wasn't working for him, but none of this was working. If she hadn't been at a neighbor's house, she would have been inside with the bomb. Rex hadn't saved her. It had been fate or luck. Or lemons, he thought, recalling what she'd been doing when her house exploded.

Detective Bell spotted them and came over, ending their conversation. The detective took one look at Rex and motioned for an EMT.

"You look like hell, Sixkiller."

"Feel like it, too." His heart had just been crushed. A heart that wasn't in love. Now he was totally confused.

"That was some tip."

"Yeah, and it took you long enough to get here." Rex took his frustration out on the other man, especially when a no-nonsense female EMT started poking and prodding at him, treating him like the annoyed, rejected guy that he was. "Why'd you wait until the bomb went off?" he accused Bell.

"You didn't say it was going to be a bomb."

"I didn't know."

Bell looked at Lisa. "You okay?"

She nodded, but she still had tears in her eyes. "Can we make the interview quick? I need to get out of here."

"Sure." Bell seemed to sense that Lisa didn't want Rex around. He more or less told Rex to get lost, nudging him toward the EMT's vehicle. "Go get patched up, and I'll talk to you when you're done."

Rex didn't like that the detective was giving him orders. But staying near Lisa wasn't helping.

When this rotten day ended, he was going to call his mom, tell her about Lisa and the baby and ask her what he should do. Maybe his dad might even have some advice. He would take whatever wisdom they doled out, which was saying a lot, considering their crummy marriage.

Regardless, they knew more than he did. They were still together after almost forty years.

He gazed back at Lisa. Her mom was by her side now, but Lisa hadn't stopped hugging herself. She stole a glance in his direction, and they stared at each other from across the chaos.

Lost in a breakup he didn't understand.

# Chapter 15

Lisa sat on her parents' stoop. She missed her porch. She missed her house. She missed Rex.

Hours had passed, but she still hadn't called him. She was nervous to hear his voice, afraid that she would cave in and agree to marry him.

If only he'd said that he loved her. If only he did love her.

"I'm sorry," she said to the baby, apologizing for not giving her a full-time father.

She glanced back at the house where her parents were. She'd told them that Rex had proposed. Her dad thought she should've accepted and her mom understood why she hadn't.

The difference between men and women, she supposed.

Realizing she couldn't avoid Rex forever, she reached for her cell and speed dialed his number.

Her heart thudded with each ring.

He answered. "Lisa?"

"Yes, it's me. How are you?"

"I'm all right, I guess."

He didn't sound all right, but she let it pass. She wasn't doing well, either. "Where are you?"

"At the station with Bell. We viewed the camera footage. Tim was on the tape, leaving a package on your porch. He tried to disguise his appearance with a baseball hat and sunglasses, but it was him. Maggie was in the background, with her hair pulled back and wearing sunglasses, too."

"So the explosive was in the package?"

"Yes. A pipe bomb with a timer. The bomb squad confirmed it."

"What's happening with my house?"

"When I left, the media was swarming around. It's already been on the news."

"I haven't been watching TV. Some reporters came here earlier, but my dad shooed them away. They haven't come back."

"That's good. Bell released Tim and Maggie's names to the press. There's also an ATL on them.

An Attempt to Locate." He paused. "I wish I could see you, Lisa."

She did, too. She itched to touch him, to soothe his bruises, but inviting him over would be a mistake. "I still need some time."

"I know. It's been an awful day. I wish I could make it better for you."

"You tried." By offering to marry her, she thought. He'd done what he'd thought was right. If only she could get past needing him to love her.

"If you want, you can call me tomorrow. We can go over to the house, and I can help you salvage anything that's left."

"Thank you." She'd already contacted her insurance company and they were sending out an agent to assess the damage. "You're my best friend, Rex."

"And you're mine."

A moment of uncomfortable silence passed between them, and she battled the ache in her heart.

He cut into the painful quiet. "I guess I should go. After I leave the station, I'm going to call my parents."

"Are you going to tell them about the baby?"

"Yes, but I'm going to tell them all about you, too."

The woman who wouldn't marry him. What would his family think? "I'll talk to you tomorrow, okay?"

"Okay." He released a rough breath. "Take care of yourself."

"I will." They said goodbye and hung up, leaving her with a lump in her throat.

Soon Lisa's mom came onto the porch, and they gazed at each other. Lisa was trying not to cry.

"Are you hungry?" Mom asked sympathetically. "I made meat loaf."

"Not right now. Maybe later."

"What about cookies and milk? Peanut butter with chocolate chunks?"

Lisa tried to smile. On any other day sweets might have cheered her up. "I'll take a rain check on those, too."

"Better get them before your dad does. They're his favorite."

"I'll come inside in a while. Maybe an hour or so. For now, I need to be by myself."

"Don't forget the little one needs to eat, too."

Lisa clutched her tummy. Earlier she and her mom had been shopping for crib sets, and now she was without a home, without a nursery and without Rex.

Was she crazy turning him down?

"I'll eat later, Mom. I promise."

"All right." The older woman reluctantly returned to the house, leaving Lisa alone.

About thirty minutes later, she heard a noise along the side of the house. Assuming it was Missy, her parents' pesky tabby that always seemed to go missing—hence the name—she got up to collect the cat.

And ran straight into Maggie.

"Don't scream," the woman hissed. "Don't you dare scream."

Lisa locked her knees to keep them from buckling. Fear shuddered through her. Why hadn't she heard their car? Or seen it? Were they parked around the corner? Had they slithered onto the property like snakes?

"Where's Tim?" she asked, barely recognizing the sound of her own chill-laced voice.

"He's over there." Maggie pointed to a shadow beside the front door. "He's waiting to see if your parents come outside."

If she screamed, would Tim do something to her mom and dad? Another blast of fear shot through her. "I'll be quiet."

"You better." Maggie seemed so different, so unlike the woman who'd taught Lisa to garden. There was nothing familiar about her. She could have been a robot of her former self, only her former self had been a lie. Nothing she'd ever said or done had been real. "We underestimated your lover. He wasn't supposed to figure out our connection to your past."

"The police are looking for you," Lisa said, hoping to use it as leverage, to catch Maggie off guard.

But her ploy didn't work.

The other woman responded, "We're aware of the bulletin. We saw a report on the news. It wasn't supposed to happen this way."

"They have you on tape. They saw Tim leave the bomb. That's how they know it was you."

"We heard that on the news, too." The blonde shifted her stance. She was dressed in casual attire and hiking boots. Devoid of makeup, her hair was slightly tousled by the breeze. "I suppose we're being filmed now, too. But it isn't live, is it? No one is watching on a monitor."

No, Lisa thought. No one was. "What do you want?"

"For you to take this." Maggie held out a pill. "And after you do, we'll go away and never come back. We can't stay here now, not with the police looking for us."

Lisa wanted desperately to scream, but not knowing what kind of danger her parents were in kept her silent.

"Take it." Maggie removed a bottle of water from her pack. "It's the easiest way."

"To kill me or the baby?"

"The baby. We realized that God wants you to live, or you would have died in the explosion."

God? They honestly thought that the Almighty

had something to do with this? How sick was their religion? How twisted were their minds?

Maggie was still holding the capsule. It looked harmless, like cold medicine, but obviously it wasn't. "Your real parents would be so disappointed in you."

Her *real* parents were in the house, unaware that a threat loomed over their heads, unaware that Lisa was in trouble.

"Take it, dammit."

Lisa reached for the pill. She would pretend to swallow it. She would do whatever she had to fool Tim and Maggie.

Then the other woman said, "If you try anything funny, I'll be forced to kill you."

Lisa nervously responded, "I thought God wants me to live."

"He does, but not if you don't get rid of that kid."

Suddenly lights flashed in their eyes.

A car came toward the house and pulled into the driveway. Lisa squinted into the brightness.

Was it Rex?

Yes, oh God, yes. It was him. She recognized his hybrid. But it seemed obvious that he didn't know that Tim and Maggie were there.

Lisa didn't have time to warn him.

Maggie pushed her hard and fast, slamming her against the side of the house. She tumbled backward, unable to cradle her fall. The capsule flew out of her hand, but it didn't seem to matter.

Instantly her stomach started to cramp, and she feared she was going to miscarry, regardless of any drug.

Tim rushed Rex as soon as he exited his car, and they tousled in the yard, back and forth, fighting over Rex's gun.

Mom and Dad heard the ruckus and came out of the house. Maggie took off running.

Dad gave chase, and Mom dashed over to Lisa.

Everything happened in a blur, like a movie being fast-forwarded in her head. Dizzy, she shivered in her mom's arms, praying that Rex prevailed.

When she saw him get to his feet, she clutched her cramping stomach. He'd knocked Tim out cold.

Dad brought Maggie back, and she was blubbering for her husband, assuming he was dead.

But he wasn't. The only one in danger of losing its life was the baby.


Rex turned his gun over to Lisa's dad, and the older man aimed it at Maggie and Tim, who was beginning to regain consciousness.

Struck with fear, Rex came over to Lisa and got on the ground with her. He'd already called 9-1-1. Soon the police and ambulance services would arrive.

She let go of her mother and crawled onto his lap. Rita stayed nearby, exchanging a nervous glance with Rex.

Lisa clung to him. "I think I might be losing the baby."

No, he thought. Please, no. "Hang in there. You'll be okay." He didn't know what else to say, other than offer his experienced support. "The Creator won't take her from us."

"What if He does?"

"He won't." Rex stroked a hand down her hair. She was breathing heavily, clearly more afraid than she'd ever been. This was worse than the threats, even worse than the bombing. This time, Tim and Maggie might have won, at least to some degree. They would be locked up, but the baby would be gone, too.

He wanted so badly to believe that *Kamama* would be born someday. Still, he couldn't help but be afraid. There was no guarantee that she would survive.

"Do you know why I came over tonight?" he asked.

Lisa shook her head. She was curled against him, as if he had the power to make her pain go away.

"I talked to my parents, and my mom said you refused my proposal because you love me, and you wanted to hear me say that I love you, too. Is that true?"

She nodded. "Yes, but you don't have to say that now just because you think you should."

"That's not why I'm going to say it. I realized as I was talking to mom that I do love you. I was confused at the bombing and wasn't able to analyze my feelings or explain why I asked you to marry me. All I knew was that I wanted to have you near me, not just as the mother of my child, but as my wife."

Her eyes went watery. "I want that, too. But what if…"

Her words drifted, but he understood what she meant. If they lost the baby, would they somehow lose each other, too?

"Nothing is going to change how I feel. And our butterfly is going to be okay." Rex was hanging on to faith, to hope, to love, just as he was holding on to Lisa.

She gripped his shoulders. "My stomach still hurts. But I'm not bleeding." She glanced at Rita, who was still on the sideline. "That's good, isn't it, Mom?"

"Yes, sweetie. That's good." She moved closer to her only child.

Rex wondered if Lisa's mom had lost babies of her own, if she and her husband had tried to have a family before they'd adopted Lisa.

"I love her," he said to Rita. "I love your daughter."

She gave him a soft smile. "She loves you, too."

"I do," Lisa offered.

She looked up at him, and he never wanted to let her go.

Emergency vehicles arrived in a blaze of sirens, with the police on their tail. As Maggie and Tim were being handcuffed, Lisa was lifted onto a gurney, and Rex rode to the hospital with her.

Praying that their baby was safe.

Lisa awakened in a hospital room with last night's chilling events still fresh in her mind. She glanced over at Rex. He was asleep in a chair beside her bed. He looked handsomely rumpled, the way one would expect an exhausted daddy to look.

God, how she loved him. He'd been there when she'd needed him most.

He seemed to sense that she was awake, and he opened his eyes, too.

"Hi," she said.

"Hi." He smiled at her.

And why not? They had a lot to smile about. The child they'd conceived was warm and snug in her womb. It had been touch and go, but in the end *Kamama* had been strong enough to survive. Their daughter was a fighter, even at this tiny stage.

"How do you feel?" he asked.

"Tired, but happy."

"Me, too." He stood up and stretched, then climbed

into bed with her. It wasn't quite dawn. The lavender light from the window was soft and beautifully hazy.

She gazed at his backlit image. "I hope she looks like you."

"She's going to look like both of us." He shifted onto his side. "I'm going to propose again, Lisa. Next time I'll have a ring, and I'll say the right words."

"You already have." She ran her hands through the thickness of his hair. "I couldn't ask for a more perfect fiancé."

"I'll sell my condo, and we can buy a house together. Or we can use the money to help rebuild yours if the insurance doesn't cover all of it. Whatever you want to do, I'm good with it."

"I think I'd like to start over in a different house." New memories, she thought. A new life.

"The first room we'll decorate will be the nursery." He snuggled closer. "Butterfly magic."

She skimmed her fingers over his jaw. "And fairies and Little People, too." She wanted their daughter to have all the magic in the world.

"I said the Lord's Prayer last night, in English and Cherokee. I must have said it a hundred times before I knew if the baby was going to be all right."

"Then you must have helped save her."

"Maybe Manny helped, too. Maybe he's her guardian angel."

"Maybe all of them are." She thought about the victims whose graves they'd visited. She would never forget them. "Someday we'll take *Kamama* to see them. We'll teach her how important it is to love everyone, no matter what race, creed or color they are."

"She's going to be an amazing kid, and we're going to have an amazing life together."

"We are," she agreed. The woman who'd made peace with her past, and the man who would always be her warrior.

Rex leaned over to kiss her, and she held him close, grateful for every moment they'd shared and every moment that was yet to come.

\* \* \* \* \*

*Bestselling author Lynne Graham is back with a fabulous new trilogy!*

PREGNANT BRIDES

*Three ordinary girls—naive, but also honest and plucky...*
*Three fabulously wealthy, impossibly handsome*
*and very ruthless men...*
*When opposites attract and passion leads to pregnancy...*
*it can only mean marriage!*
*Available next month from Harlequin Presents®:*
*the first installment*

## DESERT PRINCE, BRIDE OF INNOCENCE

\* \* \*

'THIS EVENING I'm flying to New York for two weeks,' Jasim imparted with a casualness that made her heart sink like a stone. 'That's why I had you brought here. I own this apartment and you'll be comfortable here while I'm abroad.'

'I can afford my own accommodation although I may not need it for long. I'll have another job by the time you get back—'

Jasim released a slightly harsh laugh. 'There's no need for you to look for another position. How would I ever see you? Don't you understand what I'm offering you?'

Elinor stood very still. 'No, I must be incredibly thick because I haven't quite worked out yet what you're offering me....'

His charismatic smile slashed his lean dark visage. 'Naturally, I want to take care of you....'

HPEX0110A

'No, thanks.' Elinor forced a smile and mentally willed him not to demean her with some sordid proposition. 'The only man who will ever take *care* of me with my agreement will be my husband. I'm willing to wait for you to come back but I'm not willing to be kept by you. I'm a very independent woman and what I give, I give freely.'

Jasim frowned. 'You make it all sound so serious.'

'What happened between us last night left pure chaos in its wake. Right now, I don't know whether I'm on my head or my heels. I'll stay for a while because I have nowhere else to go in the short term. So maybe it's good that you'll be away for a while.'

Jasim pulled out his wallet to extract a card. 'My private number,' he told her, presenting her with it as though it was a precious gift, which indeed it was. Many women would have done just about anything to gain access to that direct hotline to him, but his staff guarded his privacy with scrupulous care.

Before he could close the wallet, his blood ran cold in his veins. How could he have made such a serious oversight? What if he had got her pregnant? He knew that an unplanned pregnancy would engulf his life like an avalanche, crush his freedom and suffocate him. He barely stilled a shudder at the threat of such an outcome and thought how ironic it was that what his older brother had longed and prayed for to secure the line to the throne should strike Jasim as an absolute disaster....

* * *

*What will proud Prince Jasim do if Elinor is expecting his royal baby? Perhaps an arranged marriage is the only solution! But will Elinor agree? Find out in DESERT PRINCE, BRIDE OF INNOCENCE by Lynne Graham [#2884], available from Harlequin Presents® in January 2010.*

Bestselling Harlequin Presents author

# Lynne Graham

brings you an exciting new miniseries:

PREGNANT BRIDES

*Inexperienced and expecting, they're forced to marry*

Collect them all:

## DESERT PRINCE, BRIDE OF INNOCENCE

*January 2010*

## RUTHLESS MAGNATE, CONVENIENT WIFE

*February 2010*

## GREEK TYCOON, INEXPERIENCED MISTRESS

*March 2010*

Welcome to Montana—the home of bold men and daring women, where tales of passion, adventure and intrigue unfold beneath the Big Sky.

*Rogue Stallion* by DIANA PALMER

Undaunted by rogue cop Sterling McCallum's heart of stone and his warnings to back off, Jessica Larson stands her ground, braving the rising emotions between them until the mystery of his past comes to the surface.

*Montana* ★ MAVERICKS™

RETURN TO BIG SKY COUNTRY

*Available in January 2010 wherever you buy books.*

# Silhouette®
## Romantic
# SUSPENSE

# COMING NEXT MONTH
## Available December 29, 2009

**#1591 CRIMINAL DECEPTION—Marilyn Pappano**
The last person Joe Saldana expects to see again is Liz Dalton—his twin
brother's ex-girlfriend. They'd once shared an almost-moment, and the
spark is clearly still alive. But is his brother? Liz—and a slew of other
people—are looking for him, and Joe swears he knows nothing. Is he
hiding information? And when he finds out the truth about Liz, will their
reignited spark fizzle in the face of danger, secrets and lies?

**#1592 THE AGENT'S PROPOSITION—Lyn Stone**
*Special Ops*
By-the-book agent Tess Bradshaw must convince Cameron Cochran to
help her bring down a hacker threatening to shut off power across the
eastern seaboard. When Cameron decides to use her as bait, they change
her image, and the sexy makeover helps her release her inhibitions—in
Cameron's bed. Mercenaries and a hurricane threaten their newfound
passion, forcing them to choose between love and duty.

**#1593 THE PRIVATE BODYGUARD—Debra Cowan**
*The Hot Zone*
He'd died shortly after their relationship had ended, so Dr. Meredith Boren
is shocked to discover her ex-fiancé at her lake house, bleeding from a
gunshot wound. Gage Parrish has been in Witness Protection, but someone
knows he's still alive. Now Meredith is in danger, and he vows to keep her
safe. Desperate for a second chance, can he win her back before someone
kills them both?

**#1594 A DOCTOR'S WATCH—Vickie Taylor**
She's not crazy. That's what single mom Mia Serrat keeps trying
to tell everyone, but when she's hospitalized after an "accidental" fall,
Dr. Ty Hansen is the only one who believes her. Ty avoids becoming
involved with patients, but there's something about Mia that's different,
and he can't help his protective instincts when her life is jeopardized. He's
her only chance at survival, and he'll stop at nothing to save her.

SRSCNMBPA1209